HOMESICK

HOMESICK

STORIES

NINO CIPRI

DZANC BOOKS

5220 Dexter Ann Arbor Rd.
Ann Arbor, MI 48103
www.dzancbooks.org

Library of Congress Cataloging-in-Publication Data

Names: Cipri, Nino, author.
Title: Homesick : stories / by Nino Cipri.
Description: Ann Arbor, MI : Dzanc Books, [2019]
Identifiers: LCCN 2019013852 | ISBN 9781945814952
Classification: LCC PS3603.I67 A6 2019 | DDC 813/.6--dc23
LC record available at https://lccn.loc.gov/2019013852

First US edition: October 2019
Interior design by Michelle Dotter

"A Silly Love Story" first appeared in *Daily Science Fiction*, September 7th, 2012.
"Which Super Little Dead Girl™ Are You? Take Our Quiz and Find Out!" first appeared in *Nightmare Magazine*, Issue 63, Dec 2017.
"Dead Air" first appeared in *Nightmare Magazine*, Issue 71, August 2018.
"She Hides Sometimes" first appeared in *Interfictions*, Issue 7, October 2016.
"The Shape of My Name" first appeared in *Tor.com*, March 4, 2015.
"Not an Ocean but the Sea" first appeared in *The Deadline*, Issue 35, December 2015.
"Presque Vu" first appeared in *Liminal Stories*, Issue 4, October 2017.

Printed in the United States of America

10   9   8   7   6   5   4   3   2   1

CONTENTS

For my mother, Ellen, who made all this possible.

A SILLY LOVE STORY

There is something haunting Jeremy's closet.

To be fair, it's probably been in the cramped studio apartment longer than he has. He first noticed it when he moved in three weeks ago, an odd smell of apricots and old blankets that lingered toward the back of the closet. It seems content to stay in there, turning his shirts inside out and picking at the hems of his single suit. It's quiet, as poltergeists go.

Jeremy doesn't care about the suit, which he never wears. The shirts only take a few seconds to turn right-side out. He tells himself he doesn't mind.

***

"Are you going to eat the cupcake?" Merion asks.

"Yes," Jeremy says. "In a second."

"I'll eat it if you don't want it."

"You bought it for me."

"Yeah," Merion says. "But you don't seem that enthusiastic about it."

Jeremy takes a massive bite of the cupcake, fitting about a third of it in his mouth. Then, to prove he's not entirely spiteful, he gives the rest to Merion, who begins to lick away the remaining lemon-flavored frosting.

Jeremy and Merion have a standing Sunday laundry date. Jeremy doesn't need to do laundry every week, but he finds the humming warmth and clean smell of the laundromat soothing. And Merion is there, which is reason enough to go.

"Who do you think would win in a fight, Cthulu or Godzilla?" Jeremy asks, once he's swallowed enough of the cupcake to speak. He really wants to ask Merion about the thing in his closet, but isn't sure how to bring it up.

"If Cthulu and Godzilla both rose out of the sea and faced off," Merion says, "we'd all be dead. No human could withstand that kind of fight."

"Yeah, but who would win?"

"Nobody. You can't win a fight if every witness is dead."

The dryer stops. Merion gets up and opens the door, pulling pieces of clothing out of the machine and tossing them onto the cart. "It's like Schrödinger's cat. If nobody is there to see it, both Cthulu and Godzilla win and lose at the same time, for all eternity."

Merion holds out a shirt, gray with blue stripes, and adds, "I think this is yours."

Most of Jeremy's clothes are variations on the same shades of gray or blue or black. Merion, on the other hand, has the most fantastic clothes Jeremy has ever seen: brightly colored shirts, outrageously patterned pajamas, lacy bras, sparkly bowties, suspenders, soft tweed vests.

Merion is bigender, a woman sometimes and a man at others, switching out genders on a daily, sometimes hourly basis. Jeremy has eaten breakfast with Merion when she was wearing a soft, silken sundress that hugged all her curves, and then gone to the movies the same night with Merion while he was wearing a sharp-looking suit, all acute angles and honed features.

On laundry day, though, Merion is only ever Merion: jeans, a T-shirt, maybe a scarf. Narrow hips, a high forehead, an enthusiasm for morbid conversations.

They fold clothes and talk about the apocalypse—nuclear holocaust versus global pandemic, robot uprising versus alien invasion. The apocalypse is easy to talk about, existing in some hypothetical territory that is just as easy to believe as to dismiss. Jeremy doesn't mention the poltergeist in his closet. It's harder to talk about than the end of the world.

***

"Do you ever get lonely?" Jeremy asks the poltergeist, one night when he can't sleep. "Did you miss having someone around? Were you bored without shirts to turn inside out?"

There's no answer, just the lingering smell of apricots and dust. To his knowledge, Jeremy's never eaten an apricot, couldn't pick it out in a lineup of other unfamiliar fruits, so he's not sure why the smell is so identifiable. But it's definitely apricots, not pears or blueberries or cantaloupe.

"Or maybe you liked being alone. Maybe that's why you chose that closet, because there was nobody in the room attached to it. Maybe you wanted a solitary life. Afterlife, whatever."

No answer but the noise of traffic, the buzzing of the streetlight that shines too close to his window. A distant train. The creak of the overhead fan.

When he checks the next morning, Jeremy notices that the seam of his suit leg has been unraveled past the ankle. Is this an answer to his questions? A sign of affection? Of annoyance?

***

Merion is feminine today. She's wearing skinny jeans, cherry-red combat boots, a pink T-shirt decorated with cupcakes and rainbow sprinkles.

No matter what permutation of gender Merion is displaying on any given day, the cupcake obsession is a constant.

They're sitting on the floor of a Barnes & Noble, sharing a frothy coffee drink that supposedly tastes like a gingersnap cookie, but mostly tastes like sugar. Merion is paging through a fashion magazine. The smell of perfume samples wafts into Jeremy's nostrils in an unpleasant way. It doesn't go well with the aftertaste of gingersnap coffee.

Jeremy is looking at a book of nature photography. According to his mother, he's "neurodiverse." He rarely got higher than a B- in his high school classes. He failed out of art school because he couldn't write coherent essays. Words are a source of confusion and disappointment. He prefers images. Even when they lie, pictures are straightforward about being dishonest.

Merion tosses the fashion magazine onto the ground and opens up *Jane Eyre*. "I hate sad endings," she announces, to Jeremy and all the other patrons within hearing distance.

"Why?" Jeremy asks.

"They're just so ubiquitous."

"What does that mean?"

"They're too common. Sad endings have reached epidemic levels in literature. They're infecting everything, even the YA section. Even comics," she adds, pointing at the *Death of Superman* in Jeremy's pile of books, Lois Lane cradling the limp, spandex-clad body.

"I'm sure there are plenty of books with happy endings," Jeremy says, not actually that sure.

"Yeah, but they're just as bad. You know a sad ending is hovering on the horizon, just out of view, waiting to pounce on the protagonist who's finally found love or meaning or whatever."

A SILLY LOVE STORY 7

"That's why I like art," Jeremy says, studying a photo of a snow-shoe hare in the Arctic, white on white, a study in subtlety. "It never leads you on. And if it does, it's only because you let it."

Merion tosses *Jane Eyre* on top of the magazine. "Sometimes all I want to do is read a silly love story, with some kind of interesting twist. Like a kraken. A kraken is a good twist."

"Like, two krakens in love?"

"Not necessarily. Just a kraken. It doesn't need to have that big a part."

"What about a poltergeist?" Jeremy asks. "Would that be a good twist?"

Merion cocks her head, considering it. "I don't know. I'm not sure that's believable."

***

Jeremy has been in love with Merion for four weeks now, since they met at a senior art show at the Art Institute. Jeremy had just been put on academic suspension, had been given five days to move out of his dorm, and had come for the free food. Merion had worn a lavender bowtie, a dark corduroy jacket, and tortoiseshell glasses. His dark hair was slicked back, the curls reduced to subtle shining waves. There was an unlikely tension about him, something unresolved; it drew people's attention and kept them away. Jeremy had watched him from the food table, too intimidated to approach.

Jeremy was eating kalamata olives when a tall brunette with Bettie Page bangs approached Merion. "Sorry," she said. "I just have to ask, are you a girl or a boy?"

Merion glared at her. "I'm Merion."

"Like, Marion as in Maid Marion?"

"Like, Merion as in *fuck you*," he spat. Jeremy's heart had sped up. It was odd to fall in love with somebody's ferocious vulnerability, but that was the position Jeremy found himself in.

Merion walked away from the sputtering brunette, toward the table that Jeremy had haunted all night, and poured himself a plastic flute of white wine. Jeremy spat out the olive pit in his mouth and asked, "Merion as in marionberries?"

Merion turned to Jeremy with a cool, assessing look, eyebrows drawn together. "What are those?" he asked.

"Hybrid berries," Jeremy said. "They're good in pies."

And then they began talking about the genetic modification of food, whether it was a good thing that would stop world hunger and make better pies, or result in killer mutant strawberries going on a murderous rampage.

Merion invited him on their first laundry date the next day. At the laundromat, Jeremy was given the breakdown on Merion's gender: male some days, female on others, sometimes neither. Just Merion.

"Okay," Jeremy said.

"Okay?" Merion repeated. "That's it? You're not freaked out?"

Jeremy paused, searched inside himself, and said, "Nope."

"You're not going to tell me that using 'they' as a singular pronoun is grammatically incorrect?"

It sounded like Merion had gotten that argument from a lot of people. "I don't even know what a singular pronoun is."

Merion nodded. Jeremy sensed he'd passed a test. "Okay. One more thing."

"What?"

The washer dinged. Merion asked, "How do you feel about cupcakes?"

***

"What do you mean, you have a poltergeist?" Merion asks. They've left Barnes & Noble, because it seemed inappropriate to have conversations about the paranormal in a busy commercial setting. The streets at twilight, in the dim hour before the streetlights came on, were more atmospheric.

"It lives in my closet," Jeremy explains. "It's been there since I moved in."

"What does it do? Does it rearrange furniture? Or leave trails of ectoplasm?" Merion stops and puts a hand on Jeremy's shoulder. "Does it run a spectral hand down your skin while you're sleeping?"

Jeremy is too aware of the non-spectral hand on him now. "It turns my shirts inside out. And unravels the seams on my suit."

"You have a suit?" Merion asks, disbelieving. Jeremy only ever wears faded jeans, wrinkled shirts, and hooded sweatshirts. Urban camouflage.

"And it smells like apricots," Jeremy says.

"Your suit?"

"The poltergeist."

"Really? Maybe we should do an exorcism."

"No!" Jeremy says. "It's not doing anything bad, and besides, it's been there longer than I have. That doesn't seem fair."

Merion nods her agreement. "It'd be rude to evict it, I guess. Still, it's unraveling your suit—"

"Forget the suit. The suit's ugly, I haven't worn it in years. It probably doesn't fit anyway."

Merion sighs. "Have you tried to communicate?"

Jeremy shrugs. "I tried talking to it a few nights ago."

"Did it answer?"

"It tore open the seams on my pants." Jeremy thinks about it. "Maybe it doesn't like words."

"Who doesn't like words?" Merion asks.

"You can't trust words. They have too many rules, and too many ways to break the rules."

Merion looks skeptical, but then shrugs. After all, the English language isn't particularly charitable to people like Merion, with its rigidly gendered pronouns. "Maybe there's another way to communicate with it. Have you tried Morse code? What about binary?"

"Maybe I'll paint something for it." Jeremy thinks for a moment. "Let's go to the grocery store."

Apricots, as it turns out, look like small peaches, and they fit perfectly into the palm of Jeremy's hand. He stuffs a dozen into his backpack. Merion brushes one across her lips, touching the softly furred skin to her mouth.

"Try it," she says, when she catches Jeremy looking. She hands him the apricot she's been sort-of kissing.

Jeremy puts his mouth on the same spot. The fruit is cool, the fuzz ticklish against his lips. He can smell the fruit, sweet and fresh, distantly related to the musty smell in his closet.

He bites in. It's not quite ripe, and the fruit is firm and tart. He swallows and gives it back to Merion.

His heart pounds as Merion licks around the pink-yellow flesh, chews it hungrily, bite after bite. When she's done, she spits the pit into her palm and offers it to him. Jeremy wraps it in a napkin and puts it in his pocket, and they walk back outside. It's fully dark out now.

"Do you want to come over?" Jeremy asks.

Merion hesitates. Then, "No. No, I have to—"

"Okay," Jeremy says quickly. He'd rather not be lied to.

***

Jeremy sets up his easel, his acrylics, his brushes, a jar of water. He takes the frayed suit from his closet and spreads it over the milk crates he's been using as an end table. He doesn't have a big enough bowl to put the apricots in, so he uses a takeout container, piling them on top of each other. He puts the pit, a scrap of reddish-pink flesh still clinging to it, on a saucer to the side.

Jeremy doesn't usually paint still lifes. He likes to paint portraits of monsters. A bust of Cthulu. Medusa, in repose. St. George being killed by the Dragon. Fenrir devouring the world. Sometimes the monsters are ones that crawl out of his imagination or nightmares: a spider made of knives, a skeleton dressed in the skin of dead children, creatures with fangs, rotting flesh, scales, claws, hunger, rage, greed.

It is easy for him to imagine the worst things. Trying to see exactly what's in front of him is harder.

A plastic container full of living fruit. The streetlight shining through the window. The dangling thread of wool on his suit, the shiny black buttons. His cheap apartment, his silent and spectral roommate, the letter confirming his academic suspension, his infatuation with someone who switches out their gender like it's an attractive but itchy sweater, his mother's disappointment, his dwindling savings.

And the one thing he can't see, can't imagine: his future. That's the monster, really, that's lurking at the corner of this painting.

He paints for six hours, moving slowly, trying not to scare away the shy vision that's presenting itself to him. When he's finished, he gets up to wash his brushes. He stretches, trying to work the kink out of his lower back, and calls Merion. Only after the phone is ringing does Jeremy realize that it's two in the morning.

Merion picks up on the second ring.

"Is it done?"

"Do you think zombies can go through revolving doors?" Jeremy says, because it's an easier question than the one he needs to ask.

"Is it done?" Merion asks again.

"Yeah." A pause, a breath. "Will you come over?"

There's a pause. "No."

"Oh. Okay. Sorry, I'll—"

"I mean, no, I don't think zombies can go through revolving doors. Maybe one or two, but a horde of them would cause a jam." There's another pause. "I'll be over in ten minutes."

***

Merion is wearing jeans that are cut off at his knees, red combat boots, and a cowboy shirt when Jeremy answers his door. The tortoiseshell glasses are perched on his nose. There is the same odd tension around him as there was at the art opening, the air of something left unsaid.

"Let me see it," Merion says.

Jeremy opens the door and lets him in. He expects Merion to go straight for the painting, but instead, he looks at Jeremy's apartment: the beige walls, the boxes of comic books, the stacks of canvases. Unfinished.

"I'm bad at decorating," Jeremy says.

"You are," Merion agrees.

Jeremy wonders what Merion's apartment looks like. Does its decor change as often as Merion does? Is it split down the middle?

No, Jeremy decides. Merion is entirely himself (or herself, or themself). That apartment probably fits together like a Rubix cube, the same way Merion does, shifting but whole. Jeremy wonders if it's cupcake-themed.

Merion wanders over to the south side of the apartment and looks at his painting.

Jeremy stands next to him. He doesn't ask *What do you think*, even though he always wants to know what Merion thinks.

They look at the painting for a long time.

Jeremy doesn't say: *If you had to resort to cannibalism, would you eat your mother or your father first?*

He doesn't say: *Would you rather have a parasite that controlled your brain or singing mushrooms that grew out of your armpits?*

He doesn't say: *Which will happen first, will the supervolcano under Yellowstone blow up, or will the San Andreas Fault crack open and spill San Francisco into the sea?*

He says, "I think I'm in love with you."

"Okay," Merion says. Then he puts a hand on Jeremy's shoulder, turns toward him, kisses him.

His mouth is like an apricot. Closed: warm, firm, lightly furred on his upper lip. Open: wet, tart, hot.

Jeremy's knees feel a little weak, so he sits down in the chair next to the easel. Merion takes this as an invitation to sit down in his lap, straddling Jeremy's hips. His weight is heavy, pressing Jeremy deeper into the wooden chair. Pinning him there.

"What if I'm a woman underneath my clothes?" Merion asks.

"That's fine."

"What if I'm a man?"

"That's fine, too," Jeremy says.

"What if I'm neither? Or both?" Merion asks, leaning closer. The chair creaks under their weight. "Or what if I'm a monster? What would you do if I took off my shirt, and you saw scales or tentacles or tumors with tiny, scowling faces?"

Jeremy has always distrusted words. They pretend to be straightforward but shimmer like heat waves rising off the pavement. He likes images because they never pretend to be the whole story. Beyond the borders, an entire world is left to the imagination.

"I'd ask to paint you," Jeremy answers. "Merion the monster, in repose. With cupcake."

Merion laughs deep in his chest, happy.

***

In Jeremy's closet, the poltergeist pauses while pulling a shirt off its hanger. Something catches its attention, and it drifts out of the confines of the closet. It ignores the two figures sharing a single chair, pressed chest to chest, mouth to mouth; if one of them is a monster, the poltergeist doesn't care. It picks up the apricot pit from the saucer, examines the scrap of pink flesh clinging to it. It feels like a raw bone, the violent remainder of something that was torn away, chewed up, devoured.

The poltergeist hovers near Jeremy and Merion like a distant ending, ignored but insistent.

Which Super Little Dead Girl™ Are You?

Take Our Quiz and Find Out!

Everyone knows and loves the Super Little Dead Girls™! These feisty girls are all gutsy, gallant, and gung-ho about fighting monsters and undead menaces, but they've got their distinct personalities too. Take our quiz to find out which Super Little Dead Girl™ is your super alter ego!

1.) On a Friday night, where could a potential murderer or evil spirit most likely find you?

   A. At a sleepover at your friend's house, painting each other's fingernails and listening to that new boy band you're all obsessed with. You don't think about the open window, how the curtains flutter in the summer breeze like a beckoning hand, how the lamplight shines like a beacon in the dark night.

   B. In bed, covers pulled over your head and a flashlight tucked into the crook of your shoulder, a book of ghost stories resting on your legs. All of your attention is on the fictional horrors captured in printed text and inky drawings, and none is on the arcane ritual that's begun in your basement.

   C. In the graveyard by the train tracks, and yes, you know this is a bad idea, and yes, you know that Becky and her little clique were probably lying when they said they'd spent the whole night here. You're not going to back down now, though, not when she bet you five dollars.

D. Underground. You've been sleeping in the dirt for far more years than you ever walked above it.

2.) What do you hope your last act as a Living Girl would be?

A. Bargaining with the killer, telling him he can have you if he lets your friends go.

B. Writing out the name of the cult's leader in your own blood. Not that it'll do you much good; the sheriff's in on it, too.

C. Not peeing yourself when you see the red eyes glowing in the dark.

D. Forgetting. You do not wish to remember your life, and you flinch away from the shades of memory that still haunt you.

3.) What's your secret weapon?

A. You can raise other Little Dead Girls out of cemeteries, lonely roadsides, shallow graves, basements, and abandoned refrigerators. They crawl out and fight alongside you when you call them.

B. You can run your fingers along one of the spells carved into your skin, as if the scars are Braille that only you can read, and activate it. You've called down storms and ravens and blood-hungry mists to fight your enemies.

C. You transform. The sight of your scales, claws, wings, and teeth sends most bad guys running—though you like it better when they *don't* run.

D. Your voice. You speak above a whisper and can shatter a man's spirit. You speak louder than that and can shatter his skull.

4.) What's the first thing you do after becoming a Super Little Dead Girl™?

   A. Storm into the courtroom where Old Mr. Larrieux is being tried for your murder, and tell everyone who the *real* killer is.

   B. Burn your parents' house to cinders. They traded you for eternal glory in the afterlife, so they should get their reward as soon as possible.

   C. Eat Becky. You warned her to quit shoving you or something terrible would happen.

   D. Scream. You thought it was finished. You did not want to come back. Your grief levels the ghost town where you were buried more than a century ago.

5.) What's the second thing you would do as a Super Little Dead Girl™?

   A. You want to hug your parents and your little sister. Instead, you lead the police to where you were buried. You tell them the name of the man who did this to you. You narrate what he did to you in cold detail and explain where they can find him. And then you tell them to leave you alone in that ugly patch of trees off the highway where he buried you. They're too frightened to disobey. You sink to your scabby knees and dig your fingers into the loose dirt and gravel that covered your body. It feels like a thunderclap is building in your chest, and when you open your mouth, it tears out of you, echoing down the long, lonely road.

   B. You're nearly to the sheriff's house when you hear the call, and the symbols carved into your palms start to glow. You try to ignore it, but your revenge suddenly seems small, less important. Someone *needs* you. You write the sheriff a quick note on his garage door before taking his car. Your blood is tackier and harder to write with than when you died, so it's just one word: *Soon.*

C. You come back to yourself with your fingers wet with Becky's blood and your belly full and distended. Salt and copper coats your lips. You get up and start to run, impossibly fast, not even realizing that something is guiding your steps, bringing you together.

D. You accept that it's happening again. You believed it was over, that you had earned your rest. You had hoped and prayed and fought for this to never happen again. But when you hear the call, you begin to make your way toward your sisters, feeling them like warm light on your cold, papery skin.

6.) What do you have instead of eyes?

A. Crushed daisy petals and Skittles.

B. Shards of obsidian. Sometimes they fall out like sharp, black tears.

C. You actually still have eyes, but the pupils are X-shaped.

D. Windows to the Void.

7.) What's your worst subject at school?

A. Math! UGH.

B. Gym! THE WORST.

C. English! GAG.

D. Lunch. Even the other Super Little Dead Girls™ hate watching you eat.

8.) What's the worst thing about being a Super Little Dead Girl™?

A. Your parents haven't been super accepting of the new you. Actually, they can hardly bear to look at you. Whenever she sees you, your mother clutches at her chest like she has a gaping wound there that matches yours. Your father actually fainted when you came into the courtroom during the trial. They won't let your little sister see you at all, though your mom allows phone calls. You know they're scared of you, that they can't look *at* you without thinking of what happened *to* you. You want to scream at them that you're still *you,* you're still *here.* But while your screams raise the dead, they don't do much for the living.

B.   You don't like that you're always going to be a little girl. You had plans for getting older. They were sort of vague before you died: famous scientist, fabulously wealthy, married, et cetera. But since you were ritually sacrificed, those plans have gotten clearer, even as they've drifted firmly out of your grasp. You can see the woman you were going to become: the no-nonsense haircut and the sensible shoes you'd wear to the lab, the home you'd build with your spouse, with lots of land where you could walk the dogs you would rescue from the pound. It feels like the longer you're dead, the more you know about the life that you should have led.

C.   Definitely the paparazzi. These creeps follow you from school to home and even to the Super Little Dead Girl™ secret hideout. They sneak up on you and shout HEY FREAK and IS IT TRUE YOUR MOTHER HAD SEX WITH THE DEVIL. They think you're a fake. Then they think they'll outrun you. Then they think they'll be able to reach you and call you back, the sweet little girl that's still buried somewhere deep inside. They don't realize that you're not buried; you're in bloom, in control the entire time. But ugh, paparazzi taste terrible and they give you *wicked* farts.

D.   You can feel the void reaching for you, trying to drag you back to your shallow grave. You long for it as much as you

20

dread it. You reach with one hand for your new sisters, and with the other back toward the dirt where you belong. You want to rest again in that cool embrace of the grave, but your work is not yet finished.

9.) What's the best thing about being a Super Little Dead Girl™?
   A. Your friends, for sure. They're your family now.
   B. Having friends. You were kind of a loner before. (Also, the library at your secret hideout is *huge*.)
   C. Friendship, duh. (Also, free pizza from corporate sponsors.)
   D. Good company. You do not walk this path of suffering alone. (Also, the music of this century is wondrous. Rihanna and Sia "give you life," as the saying goes.)

10.) What are your future hopes and dreams as a Super Little Dead Girl™?
   A. You want to protect people—not just other little girls, but not-so-little girls, boys, and even grown-ups. You really wish grown-ups would do better at protecting other people and not, like, making more Little Dead Girls. That would make your job a lot easier.
   B. You want to know why you're all here and how this happened. You'll never grow up to be a famous scientist, but that doesn't mean you can't run experiments on your own. And you want to understand all the spells on your body, especially that one between your shoulder blades that you can't quite reach.
   C. You're going to Disneyland! No, seriously, you're going as soon as the Super Little Dead Girls™ lawyers sort through the liability issues, and you're taking the other Girls with you. You all deserve a vacation from fighting evil every other day.

D. Your job is to prepare your sisters for what is coming. They think they know horror, that they know betrayal, that they know the shadowed depths of their souls. They don't, not yet. You have read the signs, and you know the Darker Days are returning. They must be ready when the war begins again.

Mostly A:

You are Sadie! The undisputed leader of the Super Little Dead Girls™, you have a quick temper but a big heart (which everyone can see, since your killer sawed open your ribcage). You would do anything to protect your friends, and you choose justice over revenge—most of the time, anyway.

Mostly B:

You are Madelyn! You're the brainiest of the Super Little Dead Girls™ and usually the smartest person in a room. You're more cynical than some of your friends—finding out your parents are part of an evil murder cult will do that to a girl.

Mostly C:

You are Akemi! You never have and never will back down from a challenge. You're the brawn of the Super Little Dead Girls™, and the one that stretches the "Dead" part of your group's name to the limit. You've still got a heartbeat, after all—three of them, even!

Mostly D:

You are Jane Doe! You're the oldest of the Super Little Dead Girls™, the most mysterious, and indisputably the deadest. You don't open up easily, not even to your closest friends. You won't win any beauty contests, not with most of your face rotted away and all those strange extra teeth, but you're fiercely loyal and scared of nothing.

Be sure to share your results with your friends, and sign up for our newsletter to get your daily dish on the cutest and fiercest team that ever faced down necromancers, demons, and school dances. And remember: friendship never dies!

DEAD AIR

Entry 1.
[Beginning of recorded material.]
[Laughter.]

Voice: Wait, are you actually—

Nita: Time is, uh, 9:42 in the morning, September 22nd, 2013. This is Nita Rosen, interviewing subject by the name of...

Voice: Jesus, I really did not think you were serious.

Nita: So you thought I made you sign a release as, what, foreplay?

[Laughter.]

Voice: I was, like, four tequilas deep by the time you walked in and probably at five when you waved that paper in my face. I would've signed my soul away to...uh, I didn't actually sign my soul over, did I?

[Rustling paper.]

Nita: Maybe you should read this again. It's a standard release that says you're willing to be interviewed and to have this interview used in a published—well, a hopefully published art project. Thing. I'm not sure what it'll look like exactly.

Voice: Seriously? Okay. What's this project about?

Nita: It's an ethnography of the people I fuck.

[Moment of silence.]

Voice: Wow. That's. Okay.

Nita: Scared off yet?

Voice: Are you gonna play this is front of, like, some crusty old sociology professors?

Nita: It's art, not sociology. Or it's sociologically influenced art. If you read the release, there's a description.

Voice: "Documenting the erotic discourse of…" [Laughs.] This is pretentious as shit.

Nita: Duh. How else am I gonna get funding?

[Laughter.]

Voice: So if I say no…

Nita: I turn the recorder off, make us some breakfast, and shred the release form. Bid you a nice goodbye and maybe ask for your number.

Voice: Maybe?

Nita: No promises either way.

Voice: So no pressure.

Nita: That would be unethical.

Voice: I think most ethics boards would object to an author having sex with her subjects, but what do I know.

Nita: That's why it's art and not science. So?

Voice: All right. Hit me.

Nita: Okay, so time is now 9:44 in the morning, September 22nd, 2013. Do you want to be referred to anonymously, or…?

Maddie: Maddie. Pleasure to make your acquaintance.

[Laughter.]

Nita: Oh, no, the pleasure was all mine. So, first question, what's the first thing you noticed about me in the bar last night?

Maddie: Oh, wow, okay. Um. I think I saw you from the back first, so—

Nita: Was it my ass? I have a great ass.

[Laughter.]

Maddie: No! I mean, yes, you have a great ass. No, that's not what I noticed first. It was your shoulders and neck. The way your hair got stuck to the sweat on your neck when you were dancing.

Nita: Oo-kay, that sounds really unsexy but—

Maddie: I wanted to bite you. In a good way. Just put my teeth on this tendon right here and...

[...]

Nita: Mmm. That's nice. That's...yeah.

Maddie: Did you have another question?

Nita: [Clears throat.] Why did you come out last night? Were you hoping to get laid?

Maddie: I was hoping to dance, drink, have fun. Get out of my head for a while, I guess.

Nita: What was in your head that you were hoping get away from?

[...]

Nita: You don't have to answer questions you're not comfortable with.

Maddie: Okay, I'm gonna not answer that one.

Nita: Totes fair, totes fair. Were you out alone last night?

Maddie: I was by the time you got there. A couple of people I knew from work had come with me, but they went home early.

Nita: And you stayed.

Maddie: Didn't have any other plans for the night. And like I said, I wanted to, you know—

Nita: Get out of your head.

Maddie: Yeah. And get laid, I guess. I mean, I don't know if I put it like that to myself, but if we're gonna be blunt about it, yeah. I wanted to find somebody. Or at least dance with somebody.

Nita: Just like Whitney, huh.

Maddie: Who?

Nita: *Seriously?* You don't—okay, we're gonna deal with that later. But I will say that you are a serious outlier in my study, at least with your knowledge of eighties music.

Maddie: Ooh, an outlier. I like the sound of that. Though I'm curious about how many other subjects you've, uh, interviewed.

Nita: We can talk about that later, too. All right, this isn't a normal question for my interviews, but…Can I ask about, uh—

[Static.]

Nita: What the hell?

[are you sure you]

Maddie: Something wrong?

[want to]

Nita: Yeah, the recorder's being weird. Piece of crap.

Maddie: What were you going to ask?

Nita: The scars on your back. What are they from?

[…]

Nita: You don't have to answer that if you don't—

Maddie: Yeah, I'll pass. It's, uh. Not really first-date material.

Nita: Sorry. [Clears throat.] Though if you're amenable to follow-up interviews, you could give me your number.

[Laughter.]

Maddie: Shit, that was smooth. Fine. Gimme your phone.

Nita: I'm gonna pause the recording, okay? We can finish the interview after breakfast. You don't have anywhere to be, do you?

Maddie: Nowhere I'm not happy to—

[End of recorded material.]

***

Entry 2.
[Beginning of recorded material.]
[Voices, jazz music, rattling cutlery.]

Nita: Okay, so we are at Knockbox Café, Chicago, Illinois, and it is…2:24 in the afternoon, September 29, 2013. And I'm here with the lovely Maddie for our, ahem, follow-up interview.

Maddie: Follow-up interview, *my ass*. [Into microphone.] She asked me out on a date.

Nita: It's an interview! I'm recording it!

Maddie: How is this going to fit into your sex-nography or whatever if we're not actually…

Nita: In bed?

[Maddie clears her throat.]

Nita: Well, I'm not gonna make any presumptions, but like, I'm not here *just* for the sake of science.

Maddie: I thought it was art.

Nita: Sociologically influenced art.

Maddie: Let your record show that I am rolling my eyes right now.

[Laughter.]

Nita: So, I missed some of the questions on my initial interview, because a certain someone distracted me. You ready for them?

Maddie: Let me get coffee first. I feel like I'm gonna need caffeine if you're gonna ask me about my sex life in public.

Nita: Let me get your drink, okay? I promise, the imaginary ethics review board won't object.

Maddie: Okay. Can you get me a dirty chai? With soy milk?

Nita: Sure.

[21 seconds of ambient noise.]

Maddie: This is so transparently a—maybe not a date, but it's definitely a something. I have no idea why I am actually charmed by this. [Whispering into microphone.] It doesn't hurt that you're cute as hell.

[14 seconds of ambient noise.]

Maddie: It's been a long time since I felt like this. I don't know if I...

[39 seconds of ambient noise.]

Nita: Okay. So. Are you from Chicago?

Maddie: I'm from Washington. State, not DC. A tiny mountain town up in the Cascades.

Nita: What's it called?

Maddie: You wouldn't have heard of it. It's a wide spot in the road called—

[Garbled.]

Nita: ...Yeah, definitely haven't heard of it.

Maddie: Told you. Most people in Washington don't even know it's there.

Nita: What's it like?

Maddie: Used to be a logging town, now it's a ghost town. Gray and rainy. Lots of forests, lots of overgrown clearcuts.

Nita: Is it pretty, at least? With the woods and the mountains?

Maddie: I guess. *Pretty* isn't really the word I'd use.

Nita: What word would you use, then? To describe it?

Maddie: Hmmm. Fairytale-ish. But not the nice kind of fairytale. Not something Disney would make into a movie.

Nita: [Laughs.] I'm gonna nod like I totally understand what you're talking about.

Maddie: You never read the old versions of fairytales? The kind where girls drown and turn into swans—

Nita: WHAT. Wait. You're saying that [garbled] had kids drowning and—

Maddie: No! No. Just. Uh. My mom just had, uh, books when I was a kid and I—it's just the sort of place where you could imagine things happening. Like *Twin Peaks*? Have you seen that? Very David Lynch. Yeah.

[...]

Nita: Okay! Moving on. So when did you move to Chicago?

Maddie: Just this year.

Nita: From [garbled]?

Maddie: No, no, I left there after, uh. 2009. I've lived in a few places since then.

Nita: Just get restless?

Maddie: Something like that. I guess I haven't wanted to get tied down to a particular place.

Nita: Cool, I get that. Sorta. I grew up in the suburbs and then like, moved here for college. Anyway. Next question: do you still talk to your parents and—

Male Voice: I got a latte and a dirty chai with soy!

Maddie: I'll get them.

[…]

Nita: Thanks.

Maddie: Thank *you*. You're the one who bought them. So…I don't really want to talk about my parents, if that's okay?

Nita: Of course! Yeah. Like I said, this is—

Maddie: Have you seriously asked everyone that you've…you know. Slept with. Have you asked them these questions?

Nita: Yeah. I mean, it's a little less awkward when you've already, like, stuck your face in someone's pussy.

Maddie: True. I guess.

[…]

Nita: Did I make it weird? I think I made it weird.

Maddie: No, it's fine.

Nita: I don't want to make you uncomfortable. I'm just…curious. About you.

[The ambient noise briefly dips in volume. One of them breathes. The other fiddles nervously with a pen. The moment passes; conversations and the music resume.]

Maddie: It's okay. I mean. Also I don't know how to tell you this, but uh. You're interviewing the randos you take home for sex, it was never *not* gonna be weird.

Nita: [Sighs.] Yeah, fair.

Maddie: It's all right. I'm used to weird.

[…]

Maddie: What? Is there something on my face?

Nita: No, it's not…Can I just…

Maddie: What?

Nita: Would you mind if I kissed you? I just…I'm curious.

Maddie: Yeah. Yeah, all right.

[…]

[Soft laughter.]

Nita: [Softly.] Yeah, that's as good as I remember.

Maddie: Okay. Um. Did you have any other questions to ask, so we can keep pretending this is an interview?

Nita: I wasn't *pretending*! This is an actual thing. You're just.

Maddie: Just what?

Nita: An outlier.

Maddie: [Snorts.] Right. Thanks. Just what I always wanted to be.

Nita: I did have one other question. But I don't know—

Maddie: You can ask.

Nita: Well. I…so. I'm still curious? About the scars on your back?

Maddie: Oh.

Nita: What are they from?

Maddie: A car accident.

Nita: Really? They look like scratches. Like—

[Chair scraping.]

Nita: Wait, Maddie—

[Thumping, footsteps. A door opening. The sound of traffic.]

Nita: Maddie, please, I'm—

Maddie: Turn it off.

Nita: What?

Maddie: The recording. Turn it off!

Nita: All right, see, I'm turning it—

[End of recorded material.]

***

Entry 3.

[Beginning of recorded material.]

Nita: Okay, it's…1:13 in the morning, September 29th—no it's the 30th, now. Maddie just left, she said she had work in the morning so she couldn't stay. I kinda wish she had, but it's probably more than I deserve, that she stayed this long and this late. That she didn't just tell me to fuck off when we were at the café.

We talked for a long time. She told me a little bit about the car accident, and…One of her friends was in the car with her and… Maddie didn't like, come out and say it, but reading between the lines, this other girl didn't make it out. I shouldn't have been such a nosy shit, but I—

This project, like so much in my head, sounded like it would be really cool. My *ethnography*, LOL. You can't see it, but I just did really big air quotes. Why not interview the people that I fuck and then edit it all together and find some deep and underlying truth about the nature of, whatever, queer millennial sexual practices. I figured I'd end up on *This American Life* and then get like, a genius grant or something eventually. The first few interviews were cool, because yay, getting laid in the name of *art*. But this thing with Maddie is…

We've got a date for Friday, and I'm scared shitless and also hella excited. I like Maddie a lot. A lot a lot. I'm leaving the recorder at home. Wish me luck that I don't fuck things up more than I already have.

[End of recorded material.]

***

Entry 4.
[Beginning of recorded material.]
[7 seconds of breathing.]

Maddie: You're asleep right now. Which is good, because I don't know how to tell you that I don't really want to be part of your project. The ethnography of the people you sleep with. I've been having a good time with you, and I want to keep having a good time with you. Being an outlier was all right, but I think I wanna...

[Soft snore. Rustling cloth.]

Maddie: [Whispering.] Maybe it's not something I should say out loud yet. It scares me how much I've already let you in. But I really like you. I wanted you to have a record of me saying that, just in case I...

[4 seconds of soft breath.]

Maddie: It's probably too soon to be worried about that.

[Rustling cloth. Nita stirs. The sound of skin touching skin; comfort.]

Maddie: I don't want to be just an outlier, okay? Let me be something more. For as long as I can.

[End of recorded material.]

***

Entry 5.
[Beginning of recorded material.]

Voice: November. Sixteenth. Two thousand thirteen. Voicemail from phone number seven seven three—

[Garbled.]

Maddie: Hey, it's Maddie. I have a favor to ask you, and it's a pain in the ass, and I wouldn't be asking you if you weren't my last hope, but…anyway. I'm flying home for Thanksgiving and my ride just bailed on me. Do you think you could take me to O'Hare? Sorry, I know it's a pain in the ass to go to O'Hare, and my flight is at the ass crack of dawn, and traffic will probably be terrible. I will repay you with like, massive amounts of your booze of choice. You can ask me prying and personal questions and record them for the thing. Are you still doing the thing? You haven't mentioned it in a while. Anyway. Let me know. About the ride, not the thing. Okay. Bye.

Voice: End of message.

[End of recorded material.]

***

Entry 6.
[Beginning of recorded material.]
Voice: November. Twenty-second. Two thousand thirteen. Voicemail from phone number seven seven three—

[Garbled.]

Maddie: Hey, it's me. Sorry, I know it's late, just wanted to let you know I got in okay—

Female Voice: Who are you calling? Is it that girl you were telling me about?

Maddie: [Muffled.] Mom, *shut up.* [Clear.] Anyway, it's all good here. Thanks again for dropping me off at the airport.

Female Voice: Invite her too. Have her come with you when it's time.

Maddie: Mom, *stop.*

Female Voice: [Close to microphone.] Come for Christmas!

Voice: End of message.

[End of recorded material.]

***

Entry 7.

[Beginning of recorded material.]

Nita: Dear ethnography diary, or whatever this is now. Am I a terrible person? All signs currently point to yes.

I have, at this point, moved beyond Facebook stalking my outlier—listen, that was her joke at first, not mine, and I think there's a three-month minimum before you can actually call someone your girlfriend. Point is, I've moved past casually Facebook stalking Maddie and into *deep* Facebook stalking.

I wanted to look at pictures of Maddie as a kid. I just did, okay, I stand by that, I stand by my own weirdness, because yeah, when I say it like that, it makes me sound like a weirdo. But hopefully a romantic weirdo. *Anyway.* So I dug through Maddie's Facebook looking for pictures, and couldn't find any picture of her pre-2009. Nothing. And I don't know, maybe she was an ugly teenager or something or wanted to do an online makeover. But there's not even pictures that her friends posted?

And because I was bored on the Internet, and because I'm a jerk, I went and searched for [garbled], her hometown, and I couldn't even find it. And that's where it stops being sort of jerky and starts being kind of stalker-y, because then I actually went to the library and looked in an atlas, and still couldn't find it. Nothing.

[13 seconds of ambient silence. A siren passes nearby. It fades into the soft noise of birdsong, barely audible.]

Nita: I don't know why, but this feels like…a red flag? Yeah. And if it was anybody else, I'd probably ghost. Block her number, stop answering her texts. I should have renamed my project: autoethnography of a ghost. Wait, no. A ghoster? I dunno. But I've ghosted everyone that came before Maddie, and usually for similar stupid-ass reasons. Except for my high school girlfriend, because you can't really ghost someone that you had four classes with, although trust me, *I tried.*

[12 seconds of ambient silence. Nita sighs. Her breath has weight.]

Nita: This is the most masturbatory thing I've ever done as an artist. Except for that time I pretended to masturbate on stage. Ugh. Nita *out.*

[End of recorded material.]

***

Entry 8.

[Beginning of recorded material.]

[Garbled.]

Maddie: —boutique hotel, and I swear to God, they, like, origami the pillowcases and towels.

Nita: In Anacortes?

Maddie: Yeah. It's weird going there in the off season, but we had a good time.

Nita: You didn't go to your mom's place at all?

Maddie: ...I don't really like going to [garbled].

Nita: Still, it seems weird to go all the way out there for Thanksgiving and not even, like, go to your mom's house.

[...]

Nita: Sorry. That came out—

Maddie: No, I know it's—

Nita: Really didn't mean to sound that...that...

Maddie: Judgy. You sounded judgy.

Nita: Shit. I'm not judging you. I'm not, really. I'm just, like— you make me *intensely* curious, and I'm trying to like. Curb that. But it's hard.

Maddie: Thanks. I think.

Nita: I just think you're super interesting, and I know it's super dorky, but I—I really like you. And I want to know you.

[…]

Nita: Look, is this still about the ethnography? Because I promise I—

Maddie: I don't need you to promise anything, okay? That's not
what I'm asking for.

[Ambient noise. Chairs shifting on the linoleum, someone's fingers tap nervously on the tabletop. The kitchen table sounds like it
has gotten larger, stretching to a gulf between them.]

Nita: You could. Ask me to. I'd promise…shit, Maddie, I'd
promise you a lot.

[Chair scraping.]

Nita: [Closer to microphone.] Ask me to promise you something.

Maddie: [Hoarse, soft.] I don't care if you…if you're curious,
okay? I don't care if you dig up everything. But you can't ask *me*
about it, okay? It's hard enough, keeping—

[them]

Maddie: —it all out of my head.

Nita: Okay. I won't ask you.

[Sound of kissing.]

[…]

[Time is running out.]

[End of recorded material.]

***

Entry 9.

[Beginning of recorded material.]

[Traffic. Voices. The subtle rumble of an underground train.
Sparrows and starlings squawking. Bicycle bells.]

Maddie: So I've discovered how to make voice recordings on my
phone. I guess that makes this a self-ethnography. Or something.

Maybe it's just a confession? Whatever. This is weird. I don't know how you do this, Nita. I don't know if I'm going to send you this.

[23 seconds of ambient noise and birdsong.]

Maddie: I'm not supposed to—I told you that I can't talk about this. I'm not supposed to say anything about [garbled] or what happened to…

[Don't]

Maddie: They stick in my throat, even now, even here. I'm in Daley Plaza because it's the farthest place I can think of from the woods, from…

[13 seconds of ambient noise. The sound of birds intensifies.]

[say their names.]

Maddie: Nita, you think I want you to give this up because it's too personal. I don't. I want you to keep going *because* it's personal. It's been five years since I left and it's getting harder to stay away, and harder to…

[Maddie coughs harshly.]

Maddie: I…

[The sound of birds and coughing intensifies.]

[Time is…]

Male Voice: Miss? Miss? Are you okay?

Maddie: [Hoarse] I'm fine. Thanks, I'm fine.

Male Voice: Are you sure? You want me to—

Maddie: [Stronger.] Yeah, I'm okay. Thanks for—

[Come home.]

Male Voice: What was that?

Maddie: I said that I'm fine.

[Come home.]

[Footsteps.]

[Come home.][Come home.][Come home.][Come home.] [Come home.][Come home.][Come home.][Come home.][Come

home.][Come home.][Come home.][Come home.][Come home.]
[Come home.][Come home.][Come home.][Come home.][Come
home.][Come home.][Come

[End of recording.]

***

Entry 10.
[Beginning of recorded material.]

Maddie: —can't believe you never heard about this, you're the one who's always carrying this thing around.

Nita: Uh, maybe, but they didn't cover ghost-hunting in Sound Engineering for Dummies.

Maddie: It's not just for ghosts, it's for…I dunno. Anything that might have something to say.

Nita: So people just leave the recorder running and…wait?

Maddie: Leave it in an empty room and see what might be willing to speak.

Nita: Spoopy shit.

Maddie: I'm a spoopy girl.

Nita: I know. I like it. Spoopy outlier girl.

[Maddie laughs; the sound is thin, brittle.]

Nita: Now what?

Maddie: Now we leave it. Come back later and see if anything decided to leave us a message.

[Footsteps.]

Nita: Like a voicemail for ghosts.

Maddie: Not just ghosts.

Nita: Like *4'33"* for the spirit world.

Maddie: Like what?

[A door closes.]

Nita: [fainter] What? Have you never heard of— [inaudible]

[1:25:21 of ambient silence.]

[A bird calls, a harsh whistle. So loud that it might be inside the room.]

[43:57 of static.]

[End of recorded material.]

***

Entry 11.

[Beginning of recorded material.]

[Static.]

Maddie: Hi, this is Nita Rosen, coming to you live from the bedroom where I just fucked my girlfriend before trying to unconvincingly tell her that—

Nita: Oh my God, would you—

Maddie: *That!* I like, totally don't want to go to her mom's house for Christmas.

Nita: I do *not* sound like that.

Maddie: Despite the fact that it gives me the perfect opportunity to dig up all kinds of dirt about her, which is the only reason I've stayed with this freak show this long. Stay tuned. This is NPR.

Nita: Are you done?

Maddie: Oh, *fuck* no. Let me get my Terry Gross voice on. So why the sudden flip-flop, Nita? Were you getting too close to your subject? Sorry, your *outlier*? Sudden crisis of conscience, or did you just get bored and want—

Nita: Can you please turn it off?

Maddie: Oh, no. I want this on the record.

Nita: I found out who Emily is.

[9 seconds of silence. No ambient noise at all.]

[Don't say her name.]

Maddie: [Whispering.] Don't say her name.

[End of recording.]

***

Entry 11.
[Beginning of recorded material.]

Nita: One teen missing, another in critical condition after car crash in [garbled]. Underage drinking suspected as factor. The totaled car was found off Old Coach Highway in—

[4 seconds of static.]

Nita: —damage to the front and side of the car. Magdalena Lanuza, eighteen, was found in the car, several hours after the crash. The car fell from Old Coach Highway into a gully, thirty feet below the road. Lanuza claims she was accompanied by eighteen-year-old Emily Longham, who is still missing. In a statement, Emily Longham's mother, Abigail, said she believes her daughter is still out there. I'd know it if she were truly gone, she told reporters. The sheriff's office has organized a search party. Those interested in volunteering are encouraged to call the number listed below. When asked if they were looking for—

[2 seconds of static; harsh, unyielding, angry.]

Nita: —or a body, the sheriff's department gave no comment.

[11 seconds of ambient silence and static. She's weighing the past four months with what she knows now. She's thinking of long, ropey scars that rake across Maddie's spine.]

Nita: And that's it. No follow-up, as far as I can see. One girl nearly dies and another disappears, you'd assume that a small-town paper would be brooding on this shit for weeks. But there's nothing else online at all. No Facebook pictures, no memorials of this girl. I can't even find her parents. So here's the thing: this is really obviously a trauma in Maddie's past, and it looks so much more interesting than it did when I first saw those scars. And I want to find out more and I fucking hate that I do. I hate myself for looking at Maddie and seeing a...

[An outlier.]

Nita: I don't know what to do besides walk away from it. From all of it. She deserves someone who's not a…flaky weirdo artist with a voice diary. I…

[Don't.]

Nita: I don't know.

[Don't make her go alone.]

Nita: I don't know what to do.

[End of recorded material.]

***

Entry 12.

[Beginning of recorded material.]

Voice: You have reached seven seven three—

[Garbled.]

Voice: Please leave your message after the tone.

[3 seconds of silence. Nita—]

[Static.]

Nita: Hey, it's me. I'm—I don't like how we ended things last night. I want to…I don't know. I don't know what I want. I'm sorry. Just give me a call.

[End of recorded material.]

***

Entry 13.

[Beginning of recorded material.]

Voice: You have reached seven seven three—

[Garbled.]

Voice: Please leave your message after the tone.

Nita: Yeah actually, I do know what I want. I want you. I don't know what that means in the context of you and this thing about your home and—

[Don't say her name.]

Nita: —and what happened to you. And I don't know what you want, or why it's suddenly really fucking important for you to go to the creepy town that you've been avoiding for five years, and for me to go with you, but like. Okay. I don't know. I wish you would have picked up the phone so I could actually say this to you and not your—

Voice: If you would like to hear your message, please press—

Nita: God DAMN it.

[End of recorded material.]

***

Entry 14.

[Beginning of recorded material.]

Voice: December. Second. Two thousand thirteen. Voicemail from phone number seven seven three—

[Garbled.]

Maddie: Hey. It's me. I…

[Static.]

[4 seconds of silence.]

Maddie: Sorry, there's something weird going on with this connection. So, like, here's the point. You're still invited for Christmas. If you want to go. I want you with me. I don't want to be alone when—

[Static. Angry, electric buzzing. A high, sweet whistle.]

Maddie: —pick up. If you call me, I'll pick up.

[…]

[End of recorded material.]

[Sorry.]

***

Entry 15.

[Beginning of recorded material.]

[Car engine.]

Nita: Wow, it really is…

Maddie: Creepy? Dark?

Nita: Isolated. I was gonna say isolated, but yeah, those other things too. You really did grow up in the sticks. Jesus, these roads are terrifying.

Maddie: It's not the roads you have to worry about.

[…]

Nita: What the hell did you just say?

Maddie: I said you don't have to worry about the roads.

Nita: That's…that's not—

Maddie: Listen to me, okay? You'll be safe here. You're a stranger here and that's the best thing you can be.

Nita: What does that even mean? I thought this was just a family visit!

Maddie: You know it's more than that. What you need to know now— [Coughs.]

[Coughing continues.]

Maddie: [Choking.] Just be prepared okay? I…

Nita: Maddie, what's wrong? Jesus, Maddie—

[Gravel under the wheels, a clunk as the gear shifts into park. Maddie's breath is labored, whistling high in her throat.]

Nita: What is this, what's wrong? Are you having an asthma attack or something?

Maddie: [Hoarse.] It's fine. I wish— [Coughs.]

[They are only half a mile from the road where Maddie's car accident occurred.]

[They are a tiny beacon of light in dark, quiet hills.]

[They don't feel the gaze of those who are watching.]

Nita: Should I drive? These roads are scary as fuck, but I can drive.

[A door opens. Birdsong and rain. Maddie's breath smoothes out.]

Nita: Here, do you want some water?

[...]

Nita: We don't have to stay at your mom's house. We can go back to Lyndon, or even Anacortes. Fuck it, we can go back to Seattle if you—

Maddie: [Hoarse.] No. I'm all right. We're here now, we might as well…might as well finish the trip.

[End of recorded material.]

***

Entry 16.

[Beginning of recorded material.]

Nita: So. Here I am. Maddie's mom, Evie, is super nice. Her house is really pretty, up on the side of a mountain. There's a creek nearby. Lots of woods and moss, as promised. It's seriously in the middle of nowhere, though. I'm not sure what I was imagining, but…I'd originally thought that I could do some detective work while I was here. This is so embarrassing, and it's so obvious that I watch way too much TV. But I imagined myself, like, going into town and talking to the old dudes who'd be drinking coffee, and they'd be unfriendly and I'd charm them into telling me how—

[Sharp, squealing burst of static.]

Nita: What the fuck was that?

[...]

Nita: Weird. Anyway, Maddie was right, there's not really a town here. There is a gas station, which is also the post office and the hardware store. And I guess it's a movie store, too, since they had this bucket of DVDs you could rent for a few dollars each. Maddie said there's a couple churches too, but they're like, Children of the Corn meets Deliverance, you could not fucking pay me to step foot in one.

I didn't even realize that we'd passed through the town until we hit a dirt road and it got even more woodsy.

[…]

Nita: Maddie—

[Nita starts to cough.]

[The sound of the wind. The sound of birds in the trees.]

[Time is running out.]

[End of recorded material.]

***

Entry 17.

[Beginning of recorded material.]

Nita: Okay, the timestamp is uh, 8:03. Morning of December 23rd. I'm uh, I'm interviewing Evie Lanuza, mother of Maddie. [Clears throat.] Though I'm…not sure why?

Evie: Well, my daughter told me about your project.

Nita: My project? Oh, sh—she did? Okay. Uh. What did she tell you exactly?

Evie: Just that you were interested in where she'd grown up, this little town, and you know. What happened to her.

Nita: [Laughs.] Yeah, that, uh. That's basically it.

Evie: So what exactly do you want to know, Nita?

Nita: Well. Actually. Before we get started, I was wondering if you had any pictures of [Coughs.] Maddie when she was a kid. Which is probably weird, but I was just like, thinking that she must have been a really cute—

Evie: I don't. I don't keep pictures.

Nita: …Oh. Is there, um, a reason for that?

Evie. Yes.

[…]

Evie: Did you want more coffee? You look a little…

Nita: Sure. That'd be good.

[4 seconds of ambient noise, persistent birdsong and rain, and the sound of coffee being poured into an old, chipped mug.]

Nita: Thanks. So—

Evie: My husband grew up here, and even though he managed to get away to Port Townsend, he always knew he'd come back, but he put it off as long as he could. This place has a way of sinking its hooks into you.

Nita: Yeah?

Evie: He resisted coming back for so long. It almost broke us up, to tell the truth. But he came around eventually.

Nita: Yeah. Uh. Can I just ask—

Evie: Go ahead.

Nita: Where is, uh, Mr. Lanuza?

Evie: He passed on. Not long after we moved back.

[...]

Nita: That's...I'm sorry.

Evie: Oh, you don't have to say that. But I think it's what made Maddie [Coughs.]...I think that's what really soured her on this town. And then the car accident with her friend. She left soon after, and I couldn't blame her. But it's like I said. This town gets its claws into you, and it doesn't let go. I'm glad she's back. I'm glad you're here with her.

[...]

Nita: I'm going to see if— [Clears throat.] —if Maddie's awake.

Evie: Take some coffee up to her. I always loved it when my special someone did that for me.

[End of recorded material.]

***

Entry 18.
[Beginning of recorded material.]

[Footsteps. Birdsong. Rain on a dirt road.]

Nita: Okay, so I'm like…seventy-five percent sure that I'm not lost. I'm pretty sure I'm still on the road that Maddie— [Coughs.]

Nita: Fucking allergies. Anyway, the road where she had her car accident. And she was super understanding when I told her that I wanted to see it, and agreed that it was better if I satisfied my stupid-ass curiosity by myself. Well, she didn't say it was stupid, but in retrospect, it definitely was. 'Cause like, I can find my way around pretty much anywhere in Chicago, even when I'm high as fuck or drunk off my ass. But apparently I can't find my way around anywhere that's not on a grid. And of course, because it's goddamn December, the sun is buried behind the clouds. So I don't know if I'm headed in the right direction. And there's something hugely creepy about being surrounded by trees. I'm never leaving the city again. No wonder— [Clears throat.] —no wonder Maddie never comes back here. This is what I get for being such a—

[12 seconds of silence.]

[You're looking for something.]

Nita: [Whispering] What the *fuck*—

[Maybe you found it.]

[Car engine. Tires on wet pavement.]

Male Voice: Hey, you want a ride?

Nita: Uh. I think I got turned around. Do you know how to get to—

[Static.]

Male Voice: I do. But are you sure that's where you want to go? That's a lonely little spot.

Nita: I think. Yeah. I mean, I just want to see it. A friend of mine, she was in an accident there—

Male Voice: I don't need to know your business, miss. I'll drop you off there and let you find your own way back.

Nita: …Thanks.

[…]

[Radio turns on; country music. Signal fades in and out of static.]

Nita: Did you know either of the girls that were in the accident?

Male Voice: I didn't, no.

Nita: What about, uh, a Mr. Lanuza? He died, like, eight or nine years ago. I don't know his first name—

Male Voice: Listen, miss. You should keep their names out of your mouth, okay? You're a stranger here. Keep it that way.

[…]

Nita: [Faintly.] All right. Never mind.

Male Voice: That's it, over there. Careful on the shoulder, though. It's slippery from all the rain, and the guardrail's on its last legs.

[Door opens.]

Nita: Thanks.

Male Voice: Take care. And don't stay out here too long. It gets dark early.

Nita: Thanks, I got it.

[Door closes.]

[Static increases. Sounds like water, like wings, like song, like—]

Nita: —weird as it could have—

[Static.]

Nita: —so far to fall—

[Static.]

Nita: —waiting in the dark for—

[Static.]

[You should go.]

Nita: —should get going. It's—

[It's getting dark.]

Nita: Maddie's— [Coughs.] And it's getting dark.

[End of recorded material.]

***

Entry 19.

[Beginning of recorded material.]

[Voices, just on the edge of hearing. Creaking footsteps. The volume turns up, and the voices become audible.]

Evie: I like her.

Maddie: I like her too.

Evie: I'm glad you found someone who's...someone good. Strange but good.

[...]

Evie: Aren't you glad?

[...]

Evie: Do you regret bringing her here, sweetie?

Maddie: I wish we hadn't come at all.

Evie: Don't say that, Ma— [Coughs.]

Maddie: Mom, I'm—

Evie: I know you wish you could have stayed longer. I tried to—I tried to help. I thought you'd have longer. It's almost over, though.

Maddie: She doesn't know about— [Coughs.] About—

[Coughing intensifies.]

Evie: Sweetheart, shhh. You don't—

[Coughing intensifies and turns into sounds of choking.]

Nita: Oh my God—

[Footsteps.]

Nita: What's wrong with her?

Evie: She's fine, she's fine, give her some room to breathe—

Nita: Baby, it's—

Evie: I said to *give her room.* It'll pass in a minute, as soon as she—

[Choking; retching.]

Evie: Sweetheart, listen to me. You need to calm down. Clear your mind. There's mud in your mind, and you need to let the river wash it clean, okay? Let the water in and let it carry that mud away, out of your mind, out of your lungs. Stop fighting it. Let it in. The water goes in, and the mud goes out. In. Out. In. Ou—

[Vomiting.]

Evie: There you go.

[Maddie's breathing has eased.]

[Nita is crying.]

Nita: What the fuck is…

Evie: Nita, will you get some paper towels to wipe this up?

[…]

Evie: *Nita.*

Nita: Huh?

Evie: Get some paper towels from the kitchen.

Nita: Okay.

[Footsteps.]

Evie: There you go, honey. You're fine. Everything's fine. It's almost over.

[End of recorded material.]

***

Entry 20.

[Beginning of recorded material.]

[44 seconds of ambient silence.]

Maddie: Are you asleep?

Nita: No.

Maddie: I'm sorry about what happened.

Nita: You don't have to be. I'm just…God, that scared the hell out of me.

[…]

Nita: Where did that…it looked like feathers. And dirt. How did it get in your…

Maddie: Don't. Please, don't…

Nita: Don't *what?* What the fuck is happening? This went from fine to completely fucked up in like, a day, and Maddie— [Coughing, so sudden and painful that it turns into gagging.]

Maddie: Shh, baby. Stop.

Nita: I can taste it. Dirt in my mouth. You said I'd be safe.

Maddie: You don't have to be scared.

Nita: Like hell. You know what, fuck this. We should leave.

Maddie: You wanted this. You wanted to know. You kept *asking*—

Nita: Yeah, because I'm a fucking asshole who thought solving this weird-ass mystery would make good art. I changed my mind. Let's leave.

Maddie: But my mom—

Nita: Your mom is not the one gagging up mud and feathers, Madd— [Coughs.] I can't even— [Coughs.]

Maddie: Shhh, baby, it's fine. All right. We can go in the morning.

Nita: [Hoarse.] Now. Right now.

[…]

Nita: Please.

[…]

Maddie: Okay, okay. Get your stuff together. I'll tell my mom we're—

Nita: Please, don't. Just…write her a note, okay. I don't even care about my stuff, I am so fucking scared right now—

Maddie: All right, we can go. We'll find somewhere to stay outside of town.

Nita: Thank you, oh my God, babe, thank you so much. I'm so sorry I even—

Maddie: It's okay, just…just pack what you can. I'll go write my mom a note.

Nita: Okay. Okay. Yeah. I can do that.

[Footsteps.]

[A lamp clicks on.]

[…]

Evie: [whispering] Is it time?

Maddie: I…

Evie: It's sooner than I thought it would be. But it's not too late. That's the important thing. We don't want a repeat of what happened to Emily. It's better this way.

Maddie: Is it?

Evie: Don't fight it. She might still be able to get away.

[Footsteps. Rustling fabric. An embrace.]

Evie: I love you, sweetheart. Be brave. I'll miss you, but I know you'll always be close, now.

[Be brave.]

[The lamp clicks off. Footsteps.]

Nita: Did you write the note?

Maddie: [Clears throat.] Yeah.

Nita: Are you…are you okay? Sorry, I'm so fucking freaked out I didn't even think—

Maddie: It's all right. I'll be fine in a minute. [Takes a breath. Sniffs.] Are you packed?

Nita: I can't find my recorder. Have you seen it?

Maddie: Maybe it's in the car.

Nita: Why would it…you know what, I don't even care. Let's just get the fuck out of here.

Maddie: All right. Before we go, can I just…

[It's a goodbye kiss, but Nita doesn't know that.]

Nita: Ready?

Maddie: Yeah.

[Footsteps. A door opens and closes. The sound of night: wind slapping against wet leaves, rain hitting gravel. The car doors open and shut, and the engine turns on. So does the radio: nothing but loud, angry static.]

Nita: Fuck!

[The radio shuts off. The car shifts into gear, and then gravel crunches under the tires as they start to drive.]

[4:21 minutes of ambient noise.]

Maddie: I'm actually grateful, you know. That I came back. That you got me to come back.

Nita: You were right. I shouldn't have kept asking you. It was—

Maddie: I needed to do it. I'd put it off for so long.

Nita: Put what off?

Maddie: I'd almost forgotten. You woke something up. Your questions.

Nita: Mad— [Coughs.] What are you talking about?

Maddie: It was almost too late.

[…]

Nita: Look, I'm already freaked the hell out, so if you could do me a favor and not be all fucking cryptic—

Maddie: Remember what I said when we were on our way here? You're safe. You're safe because you're a stranger. You're right to want to get out of here as soon as you can. This place…it does something to you. Doesn't matter how far you go, it's always pulling you back. That's what happened to my dad, and it was—Emily knew there was no point in trying to get away, but I insisted, and she—

Nita: Ma— [Chokes.]

Maddie: Don't. It's okay. Don't try to fight it.

Nita: Fight what? Jesus, what…

[The engine has grown louder.]

Nita: Can you slow down?

Maddie: It won't change what happens next.

Nita: Oh my God. Please, whatever you're thinking of doing, please don't.

Maddie: I am so lucky I met you. I'm just—I always thought I'd be alone, and that nobody would know my name. I'm so grateful that you're here.

[You're here.]

Maddie: Try not to think about me, okay? Just leave me behind. Don't even say my n—

[The crash through the guardrails takes them both by surprise. They scream the entire way down. A scream with shattered glass and scraping metal; a scream that wrenches itself open from the inside. A scream infused with something inhuman, old as mountains, wild as a bird suddenly breaking from a cage, electric in the air. A scream with blood on its teeth.]

[End of recorded material.]

***

Entry 21.

[Beginning of recorded material.]

[1:32 minutes of ambient noise: traffic, voices, dogs barking.]

Nita: Timestamp. It's, uh, 3:28 in the afternoon. January 10th, 2014.

[...]

Nita: I'm moving out tomorrow. Um. I can't really do stairs that well, at least until the leg brace comes off, so I'll be staying at my mom's. I'm just here to grab some clothes and things. And to leave this recorder on.

[...]

Nita: I guess what I'm saying is, if you have anything else you want to say, I'll be listening. I'll leave the recorder on in the empty room. Let it run until the battery dies, I guess.

[...]

[Footsteps, uneven and limping. A door creaks as it closes.]

[...]

[...]

[...]

[...]

[

.

.

.

]

[Are you sure you want to hear what we have to say?]

SHE HIDES SOMETIMES

The linen closet disappeared first. Or maybe it was just the first thing that Anjana noticed the morning her parents moved into the nursing home.

The closet was downstairs, in the short hallway between the kitchen and the guest bedroom. It was narrow, hardly wider than Anjana's shoulders, with two high shelves inside. It had always seemed like such a superfluous closet, so far away from the bedrooms upstairs. Too far from the kitchen to be a pantry. Too far from the front door to store jackets and shoes.

Anjana was trying to find a bedspread that Auntie Priya had sent them from Dhaka, the white one with the blue and green embroidered flowers. She thought it might cheer up her parents' suite in the nursing home. She could bring it to them that weekend, before she went back to Pittsburgh and school. The bedspread had been her mother's favorite before she'd fallen ill.

Her father was a surgeon, and her mother had been a teacher, and they had been a family that loved clear answers and facts, truths that were clipped and groomed into manageable, sensible creatures. Her mother's sickness was not like that: it was feral and strange. It had no name and no diagnosis, just a list of symptoms that added up to a woman Anjana no longer knew. Pale-skinned, a blank stare, her hands curling restlessly against her thighs. Her face had sunken, and her hair was kept in a loose, fraying braid—Dad's handiwork. For a former surgeon, he could be remarkably imprecise with his hands. He hadn't bothered to pluck her eyebrows either, or the small dark hairs on her chin and upper lip. Her mother would have hated being seen like that.

Just that morning, after they'd packed up the car, Dad had sent her into the house to fetch her mother. She'd found her in the master bedroom, one hand resting on the armoire—it was too big to take with them, and none of their friends or relatives wanted it. Her head was cocked, as if she were listening for something.

"Mom," Anjana said gently. "It's time to go."

Her mother had rested her palm against the armoire's carved wooden door, and said, "She hides sometimes."

Anjana had often hidden in there when she was a small child. She'd burrowed all the way into the back, nestled amongst her mother's saris and her father's suits. She'd leave the door just slightly ajar and breathe as quietly as she could. *Come and find me!* she'd call to her mother or sister, when she was in the mood to play. Other times, she just sat in there, silently hidden away. Safe.

Anjana had cursed her father for making her do this alone, for staying in the car. "She's not there now, Mom. Come on. We're leaving."

When her mother didn't move, Anjana wrapped her hand around her arm, tried to tug her away. Her mother shook her off and shouted, "*Where is she?*"

Anjana had taken a step back, voice shaking. "We—we'll go find her. Please, come with me."

Her mother had glared at her. Then she'd turned on her heel, walked out of the room, down the stairs, and out the door without stopping to put on shoes or her coat.

Anjana touched the peach-colored wall where the closet had been. She thought of the handprint her mother had left on the armoire upstairs. She'd dusted, cleaned the windows, scrubbed the floors, and stripped the bed, but she hadn't been able to bring herself to wipe away that small mark, the last place in the house that had felt her mother's touch. She'd come down here instead, to look for the bedspread from Auntie Priya.

Anjana briefly thought of calling her father, asking if he'd gotten rid of the closet during a remodel, then she decided against it. Dad had enough to worry about already.

***

The entrance to the attic disappeared next. Anjana wasn't even looking for it, but on a trip to the bathroom, she happened to look up. The square wooden panel had been replaced by smooth ceiling. She blinked. Went to the bathroom. Urinated. Washed her hands. Came back out and looked again. The ceiling was still smooth. She went back to cleaning the windows in the living room and told herself that she was very tired and under a lot of stress. She'd finish cleaning the living room and then go to sleep. The attic would be there in the morning.

It was not there in the morning. And the small bay window in the kitchen, where she and Chitra had often done homework while their mother prepared dinner, was gone as well. The little nook with the cushioned bench had been walled over and fitted with a square window, small and cramped like the window to a jail cell. There was no way her father would have remodeled the kitchen to get rid of it. But she called him anyway, to make sure.

"How's Mom?" she asked, the customary opening of all their conversations for the past few months. They talked about her, around her, over her. Anjana couldn't remember the last time she'd talked *to* her mother. If she'd known it was the last time, she would have made an effort to remember.

A shuffle of breath, or perhaps Dad was shifting the phone in his hand. "She's okay," he said.

What was that supposed to mean? Anjana decided that it hardly mattered. "And how are you, Dad?"

"I'm adjusting."

He sounded sorry for himself, and it made Anjana grit her teeth. He wasn't after her guilt or her sympathy. He had made his choice to go with his wife into a nursing home, to spend whatever time they had left together. If he had regrets, he hadn't voiced them. He just sounded miserable, and there was nothing Anjana could do.

"That's good," she said, and could think of nothing else to add.

"How's the house?" he asked, still glum. "How are you getting along with it?"

She nearly laughed, hysteria edging up on her. "It's okay," she said. "I meant to ask. Did you remodel before Mom got sick?"

"Remodel?" he asked. "No. Why?"

Anjana had learned how to lie to her father long ago, and it was effortless now. "Just wondering," she said. "I thought the light fixtures seemed different."

She cleaned the kitchen that day, avoiding the wall where the little nook had been. She managed to lose herself in packing up her parents' cookware and plates so she could take them back to Pittsburgh with her. When she opened the door to the garage to pack the boxes in her car, she discovered that it had shrunk from a double to a single. She could hardly open the doors to her Prius. She moved her car out into the driveway.

***

When she called Chitra, it was nearly midnight. Not that it mattered: Chitra was in Sacramento, three hours behind, and Anjana
needed to tell someone that the basement door had disappeared.

"I think Bobby's having an affair," Chitra said by way of greeting.

Chitra's husband had probably had several affairs, but Anjana
knew better than to say this. Her role was to listen as Chitra laid
out all the evidence of Bobby's possible infidelity, to make sympa-
thetic noises in the right places, and to call Bobby things like *shit-
weasel* and *douchecanoe*, since it would make Chitra laugh. They'd
honed the routine years and several boyfriends ago. But Anjana
couldn't do it.

"I can't find the basement," she said. She was sitting on the floor
in the living room, willing herself not to look over her shoulder. Every time she did, it seemed like the walls had inched closer to her.

"What can't you find in the basement?" Chitra asked.

"No, the whole basement. I can't find it anymore."

There was a crackly silence. The sound of all the miles between
them, between their childhood home and Chitra's grown-up life.

"I'm sorry, what?" Chitra said.

*The basement is gone. The kitchen nook is gone. The attic and the
linen closet and who knows what else. The house is disappearing in small
slices.* Anjana said none of that.

What she said was, "Never mind, it's not important. What did
Bobby do this time?"

Anjana remembered how their mother would sometimes listen
to Chitra's phone calls on the extension in her own bedroom, before
they all had cell phones. Mom would hold a hand over her nose and
mouth so that Chitra couldn't hear her breathing. Anjana, who was
seven years younger than Chitra, would watch from the same spot
that she was sitting in now, pretending to read *Animorphs* books and
spying on her mother, who was spying on her older sister. *Was Mom*

listening to me talk to Katie? Chitra would demand later, and Anjana would flush and shrug and say, *I don't know, I was reading.*

Anjana could have made a noise, could have told. But she'd let herself be invisible instead. Complicit.

"Maybe I should come home," Chitra said. "Bobby can sit and stew on his own for a few days, and I can help you get the house together to be sold."

"No!" Anjana cried, though she wasn't sure why. "No, that's okay. I mean—"

"No, you're right. I was always useless at stuff like that. I'd probably just get in your way."

Anjana had to bite her lip. Some kind of feeling was bubbling up, tight and hot and slippery, trying to pull itself out of her throat.

***

Anjana decided she would continue sleeping in her bed. She brushed her teeth and washed her face believing that she'd be able to do it. She walked into her room and sat down on her old bed, looking around with relief. Her room, at least, was the same, still burdened with remnants of her childhood. The walls were the same pale blue that Dad painted on her thirteenth birthday. The bookshelf still had an entire shelf devoted to *Animorphs* and *Yu-Gi-Oh!*

Anjana wrapped her arms around her knees, shut her eyes, and tried to listen to the house the way she used to, when her sister was already grown and her parents existed on the other side of a great impassable wall: in their late forties when she was born, from another generation, from another country.

The house didn't sound different. It sounded the same as when she was a child, a little girl who had liked to hide sometimes. She'd burrowed into a quiet, tight-fitting spot, held her breath, and tried to imagine what the world would be like if she disappeared.

When Anjana opened her eyes, she went cold with fear. The bookshelves were gone. The closet door hung ajar, empty. The walls had crept closer to her. It took several moments before she could force her limbs to move, to gather up her pillow and duvet and walk—calmly, slowly, as if she were trying to escape the notice of a predator—outside to her car, still parked in the driveway. She slept fitfully in the backseat, her breath fogging the windows.

***

"Put Mom on the phone," Anjana said, the next morning when she called her father.

Dad sighed. "It's not a good day."

Anjana had been awake since dawn. She'd walked through the house, taking in the changes. The back patio was now a small, cement stairway to the garden. The dining room had shrunk, and the tables and chairs crowded against each other. Chitra's old bedroom, the one her parents had converted into an office, had disappeared entirely.

"I want to talk to her."

"Anjana, I'm not even sure she'll hear you."

"There's nothing wrong with her *ears*, Dad!" she shouted into the phone. "I know her fucking mind is gone, but she can still hear me when I talk to her!"

Reproachful silence; a specialty of her father's. Whereas her mother could shake the walls, each word an earthquake, her father retreated into a silence that vibrated in the air.

Anjana belonged as much to one as to the other. Various boyfriends had told her as much. So she waited for her father to say something, but when he did, it was a shock.

"I talk to her every day," he said. He sounded old, as old as death, as old as sadness itself. "And..."

Anjana bit her knuckles waiting for him to finish, but the silence seemed to collapse on itself. Hysteria crept up on her. "Dad?" she said, suddenly convinced that he, too, had disappeared.

"I'll see if she's sleeping," he said eventually. "I'll call you back."

Anjana walked through the house again. The dining room was now hardly bigger than a walk-in closet. The big mahogany table and matching chairs were gone. It made Anjana feel dizzy, nauseous. Where were the rooms going? Why didn't they make a sound as they disappeared?

The stairs had narrowed, and Anjana's shoulders brushed the sides. She tripped at the top, expecting more steps. How many had there been? Was the ceiling hanging lower than it used to?

The master bedroom had shrunk, and her parents' stripped bed pressed against the wooden armoire. The attached bathroom had vanished. The room even smelled different. It was missing the top notes of her parents' presence: her mother's amber perfume, her father's cedar aftershave, laundry soap and hospital antiseptic, the tea they both drank. The room smelled as if nobody had breathed in there for years.

The phone in Anjana's hand buzzed, and she nearly dropped it.

"Dad?" she said, sitting down on the stripped bed.

"I'm with her now," her father said. "If you still want to talk to her."

"Is she..." Anjana trailed off, not sure how to finish. *Is she even there?* She remembered her last conversation with her mother, in this same room, only three days ago.

"I'll hold the phone to her ear, as long as she'll let me. She might not. We'll see what happens."

"Okay, Dad," Anjana said, and then added, "I'm sorry I shouted before. I love you."

"I love you, too. Here's your mother." And then, quieter, he said, "Taslima? It's Anjana. It's your daughter. She wants to talk to you."

For a long second, Anjana only shut her eyes and listened to her mother's breath, a sound as familiar as the house used to be. In, out. Pause. In, out. Anjana breathed with her and thought of the work her mother had put into the house: cleaning it and decorating it and inviting others into it, making it warm and welcoming. She'd set down the tiles in the master bathroom, sanded and varnished the dining room table, put together the shelves in Anjana's bedroom. All of them gone.

"Mom?" Anjana said, and then cleared her throat. "Mom, it's me. It's Anjana."

Just her mother's breath. Was that all that was left of her?

"There's something happening in the house. To it, I mean. I can't—" She lowered her voice, wondering if her father was listening in. She didn't want him to hear. "I can't find parts of it. The basement is gone. So is the linen closet and the kitchen nook and my bookshelves. It's disappearing. Oh, Mama," she said, and choked on the sound, the name of the first home any child ever knew.

"I don't know what's happening," she cried. "I'm not crazy, but I don't know where it's going."

She was in her parents' bedroom, a room once as familiar as her own. She'd slept in here when she was a baby, in a crib next to her parents' bed. She'd crawled in here when she felt ill, and read books inside a cocoon of blankets on the bed. She'd peeked in her parents' dresser, trying to find the hidden aspects of them. And she had burrowed deep into the armoire, touching her father's suits to her cheek, opening shoe boxes, rubbing her mother's dresses and scarves between her fingers.

And now, even the way sounds echoed and air moved was different. Was *wrong*.

"Mom, I don't know what to do," she said. "I can't tell Dad or Chitra. But I don't know how to stop it. Tell me what to do."

Her mother said nothing. Anjana might as well have been speaking to the empty house.

She couldn't stand it. She stumbled down the stairs and outside onto the cement block that had insinuated itself where the patio should be, sat down on the bottom stair, and cried. It took her a few minutes to notice her father's voice calling her name.

"I'm sorry," she said. "Sorry, Dad. I'm all right. I just—"

"She's trying to say something," he said, cutting her off. "I don't know what, but..."

"Put her on again," Anjana demanded.

There was a low murmur of sound. Anjana shut her eyes, listening, desperate to hear whatever her mother might say, even as she told herself that it might be nothing, or it might be nonsense.

"Mom?" she said softly. "Mom, I'm here. I'm listening."

The murmur persisted.

"Did you hear? She said your name," Dad said. "Taslima? Do you know who you're talking to?"

Inhale, exhale. Pause. "Anjana. Baby Jana."

Anjana shut her eyes and took her own shaky breath. "Hi, Mom. I miss you."

"Where did you go?" Mom asked. "Miss you too."

***

Half an hour later, Anjana finally said her goodbyes to her father, who had cautioned her—and himself—not to get their hopes up. A single instance of clarity didn't mean she was getting better.

"I wish Chitra could have heard her," Dad said. "I wish..."

"I know," Anjana said. "Me too."

When they finally hung up, Anjana dropped the phone on the cement deck beside her and buried her face in her hands. Her long dark hair hung over her eyes, shutting the rest of the world out.

When she lifted her head, the sun had nearly set, and it was getting dark.

She sighed and glanced back at the house. It looked so normal from out here. It almost gave her hope that the inside would be restored and whole again, that the same magic that had momentarily brought her mother back would bring the house back as well. She got up, feeling sore and wrung out from crying, and let herself back inside.

The kitchen was stripped and empty, lit only by a bare bulb. The living room was the same, cleared of furniture, shrunken and shriveled like a fruit left to dry in the sun. Anjana swallowed down a scream, suppressed the urge to run back outside. She climbed the stairs that were narrow and steep. Upstairs, the hallway was cramped and tight, and all the doors stood ajar, peeking into small, barren cells.

Except in her parents' room, where the armoire still stood. It was covered in dust, as if it had been abandoned years before. A silent witness, a warning.

Where did you go, her mother had asked. Anjana shut her eyes. Her fingers found the latch of the armoire and turned it. The hinges squealed. The inside was the way it had always been, full of her parents' clothes, smelling of varnished wood, muslin and silk, shoe polish.

Her grownup body was not too big to fit inside, or maybe the armoire was shifting and stretching to accommodate her. Perhaps she was shrinking. She burrowed to the very back, behind her father's suits and her mother's many scarves, the wood creaking under her weight as she settled in. The armoire stretched and grew around her, growing as big as the house had once been.

The door to the armoire closed, shutting out the gray light. The latch clicked.

"Come and find me," Anjana whispered.

LET DOWN, SET FREE

Dear Bobby:

I figure you'll be the first person they'll call. The ink's barely dry on our divorce papers, after all, and you're still listed as my next of kin. Hell, the state hasn't even sent me the new house title yet, the one with only my name on it, all by its lonesome self. In some bureaucratic parallel universe, we're still living together in wedded bliss.

Now, I told myself that this letter wouldn't be bitter, but that's probably a lie. I told myself that it would be straightforward, and then laughed at the audacity of *that* fib. You always liked to accuse me of talking around things, and I never could disagree with you. But that's the nice thing about a letter: it provides a captive audience. No interruptions, no impatience, no eye rolling. You're going to damn well let me tell this story in my own time.

So here's the first thing: the floating trees. Have you been following this story? I wasn't, though I know more about them now, obviously: big-ass seedpods that look just like a milkweed fluff, with a network of flat, feathery branches, dense as a cloud and just as light. More of them after every full moon, like inflatable oak trees floating through the air with the greatest of ease. They've been spotted everywhere from the Carolinas to Florida, but nobody's sure exactly where they're coming from or what kind of plant they grow into.

Personally, I was too busy being miserable to pay much attention. Getting a divorce didn't leave much room for other concerns. When you see the rest of your lonely life stretching out ahead of you like rusty railroad tracks, everything else sort of fades into the background. Until this afternoon.

I still take my walks up to the cliffs by the river every day, just after lunch. It clears my head. The house is too quiet now that nobody's playing godawful hillbilly music by some hack that should be shot for his crimes against the mandolin. Anyway, I was on the part of the trail that butts up against the Morgan's property when I spotted a floating tree in one of their pastures. Some of the branches were caught in the fencing wire. It had thoroughly spooked Nancy's quarter horses, who had fled to the far side of field, snorting and eyeballing the invader.

I had to let Nancy know. It was only neighborly, after all. I know I'm not much of a neighbor, but Nancy's been sending her grandnephew over to mow the front yard, since it became apparent I wasn't going to do it after you left. Half the neighbors avoid me, like having your husband run off with one of his interns is a contagious disease, while the others keep offering to set me up with bachelor cousins or uncles. Nancy just sends over a fine-looking college boy to mow my lawn bare-chested once a week. Bless that woman.

Nancy opened the door, and after exchanging the necessary pleasantries about the lovely spring weather, I told her, "There's one a-them floating trees in your east pasture. The horses are pretty spooked."

"Oh, sugar," said Nancy. "Let me get my boots on."

We walked together back to the pasture, chatting amiably about her grandnephew and the price of gasoline and what-all else. I do still love the way Kentuckians talk, sweet and smooth like their whiskey.

We crested the slight rise, and Nancy jumped a little when she saw the tree, caught against the fence.

"Oh!" she said. "Oh, it's so…"

She couldn't seem to think of an adjective, and neither could I, so I nodded and said, "It sure is."

Even though I can describe all the features of a floating tree, it's hard to describe how this one made me feel. I'd seen footage of them moving through a landscape of blue sky and clouds, but the shots don't give you any sense of their enormity, or how it was constantly in motion, straining to catch the smallest breeze. The tree had *presence*.

"It's lovely," she said, and I could tell she meant it, that she felt the same way I did. "I didn't know they were so…"

"Me neither."

"It seems such a shame to burn it," she said.

"What? Burn it?" It seemed like blasphemy, Bobby. More than that, it seemed cruel.

"Well, sure, honey. That's what the government said to do if one landed on your property. Call it in to some hotline and then burn the thing so it don't germinate."

It seemed like one thing too much. I could handle the divorce, the quiet of the days and nights spent alone. I could handle knowing I'll probably die a lonely old woman, stuck in the house I won as a consolation prize for our failed marriage.

But I could not stand to let this tree go up in flames just because the wind died in the wrong place. I'd have rather seen our house burn down—all the last reminders of the years we scraped some happiness together—than that tree.

"Don't," I said. "Don't call it in. I'll take care of it somehow."

Nancy looked at me, probably thinking that I couldn't even take care of my own damned lawn without her help. But she put up both her hands and said, "Tell you what. I'm gonna move my horses over to the north pasture. Get it out of my fencing wire and then we'll figure something out."

It took me twenty minutes to untangle that thing from the fence. The seed felt warm in my hands, probably from sitting in the sun. Its branches waved and rustled above my head. What would it be like, I wondered, to see it planted? What kind of soil did it need to set down roots? What would it grow into?

My hands on the smooth, wrinkled casing of the seed; my fingers wrapped around the rough bark of the trunk. Tell you this, Bobby: it felt like touching a lover for the first time. Not in the heat of sex, but in that giddy flush when you realize you *can* touch someone, as much as you like. Now you've got permission, and you can run your hands over his shoulder or slap him on butt when he gets fresh while you're cooking dinner.

After I got it free, the wind picked up, and the seed nearly lifted itself out of my arms. I latched onto it, and it damn near pulled me off my feet.

I suppose that's where I got the idea. Where the seed of it germinated, you might say.

(I always hated your puns, Bobby, but I find I miss them.)

I looked up into the sky through those gray branches, with that seed pressing warm against my belly and chest, and I felt like—well, the way I'd felt with you, about a million years ago. Young and alive and ready to make some real questionable choices.

"Melissa," Nancy said from behind me. "You get that tree free yet?"

I suppose I don't have to tell you that I was a little embarrassed to be caught feeling up a floating alien tree.

"It nearly got away from me," I said.

Nancy came and stood next to me. "I thought that was the idea."

I looked back up into the crown of the tree, feeling all jumbled up inside. "It should be free," I said.

"It'll just set down in someone else's yard," Nancy said. She was carrying a leather lead in her hand, and she swung it against her leg thoughtfully. "Seems a shame."

"A damn shame," I sighed. Then I confessed, "I'm getting an idea. A real dumb idea."

"Are you, now," Nancy said. "'Cause I think I'm getting a similar one."

We looked at each other, two old women standing in muddy meadow. And after a second, we both grinned. Nancy handed me the lead, and I lassoed it around the trunk of the tree. Together, we towed it back to her barn.

When Nancy offered me "Tea, or something stronger?" I took her up on the latter. We sat on her front porch, drinking her husband's bourbon. We'd roped the tree behind her barn, hidden from the road, and I could just see the tops of its branches.

"It's picking up some," Nancy said. "The wind."

I nodded. I'd noticed.

"I got an old saddle I wouldn't miss," she added, like she was just making conversation.

"Lord, Nancy." I set my glass of bourbon down. "Are we really gonna go through with this damn fool idea?"

"Not we, girl. Just you. God knows I can barely keep my seat on a horse these days, and they're stuck on the ground. You're young enough to make it work."

She didn't add anything else, but I know what she was thinking: she had Tom to think of, and her kids, and the nieces and nephews and grandnephews and all. If I got killed, only you and Nancy would mourn me. The rest of my family would think it's only what I deserved for running off with a balding hillbilly from Bumblefuck, Kentucky.

(Mother's words, dear. Not mine. I always thought your receding hairline made you look sophisticated.)

I had nothing and nobody. And instead of feeling trapped by that thought, God help me, I felt freed by it.

"I'll fetch that old saddle soon as you're done with your drink," Nancy said. "You can get the wheelbarrow out of the barn."

I went home long enough to pack a little bag: granola bars, raincoat, wool blanket, all the rope I could find, and the emergency bottle of Pappy Van Winkle. If I was going to die doing this crazy thing, I sure as hell wasn't going to die sober, nor drunk on the cheap stuff.

The moon was coming up as we wheeled the seed up to the cliffs that overlook the river, the moon just a few days past fullness. It took ages to get there, trying to keep the tree's branches from getting tangled up in the maples and oaks along the path. Each step we took, I tried to talk myself out of this stupid, dangerous plan. I'd likely kill myself. At the very least, I was probably breaking some law or another, and it was impossible to think nobody would notice. And yet, we kept walking, listening to the music of the hollow branches rustling.

By the time we arrived at the cliffs, the moon was high above the horizon, and the sun was just sinking below it. Come summer, these cliffs will be populated with local teenagers. They'll sunbathe, dare each other to jump into the water. Maybe some of them will sneak back here after dark to get drunk, fool around. You and I walked up here together when we were first looking at buying the house, and again just after we'd bought it: we made love just like teenagers, only with better booze and less fumbling.

But it was never our spot. It was always mine, where I took my bad moods and suspicions and tears. Now it was where I carried a strange invader, a tree-sized seedpod that even now was catching the strengthening wind.

I set the seed down on the ground, only a few feet from the edge of the cliff, keeping one hand on the rope we'd lashed around the trunk like a pair of reins.

"Ready?" Nancy said.

"Like hell," I answered. She held out her hand, and I took it. The old hag even had the gall to slap my butt as I got into the saddle we'd roped to it.

We sat there, the tree and Nancy and I, considering the edge of the cliff.

"I feel like a damn fool," I said. I touched the tree for reassurance, trying to pull back some of the warm glow that had infused me back in the pasture. Lord, maybe this was why the government was telling people to burn the things. The trees got inside your head, inspired you to all kinds of foolishness.

"Well, you look—"

I never got a chance to find out what Nancy thought I looked like. A gust of wind picked the tree and I up and tossed us into the air.

I screamed as we tumbled over the edge of the cliff. I shut my eyes, pressing my face into the seed's trunk, the stiff fibers scratching my face. I might have peed myself the tiniest bit.

Then I realized I wasn't falling. I opened my eyes, still clinging to the trunk, and looked cautiously around. We were floating, a few dozen feet above the river, level with the canopies of all the earthbound trees rooted below. As the wind picked up, the seed tilted, catching the passing breeze in its branches, lifting us higher. I sucked in lungfuls of the night air as we drifted, my weight apparently negligible in the strong wind.

Nancy was whooping it up on the cliff, just like one of those teenagers. As I looked back and waved, she fell onto her butt, hands at her mouth. She got smaller and smaller, then disappeared entirely.

I have never held to it when people say you should never look back. When we took off, the tree and I, I craned my neck until I could see our house—it's still ours, even though that new deed is probably in the mail. It looked tiny from up here. All those times when I'd rattled against its walls like a marble in an otherwise empty box, they shrank in my memory as the house shrank in my sight, and eventually, they'll both recede into nothing at all.

We left the river behind and floated onwards, on a northeast bearing. Now, we're floating above the green Kentucky hills that you love so much. Bathed in the moonlight, they look as beautiful as you always said they were. Even the gray fields of soybeans, rusted trucks propped up in dirt driveways, trailers that probably double as meth labs, and giant Wal-Marts with acres of asphalt parking lot: they're all lovely, given a little bit of distance and a healthy dose of moonlight.

When we do set down, if it's a good enough place, I've got a mind to dig a hole for this seed, to cover it over with dirt, and see what grows. And I'll tell you this: I feel a lot lighter than I did when I was on the ground.

Not all my love, but probably more than you'd guess,

Melissa

THE SHAPE OF MY NAME

The year 2076 smells like antiseptic gauze and the lavender diffuser that Dara set up in my room. It has the bitter aftertaste of pills: probiotics and microphages and PPMOs. It feels like the itch of healing, the ache that's settled on my pubic bone. It has the sound of a new name that's fresh and yet familiar on my lips.

The future feels lighter than the past. I think I know why you chose it over me, Mama.

***

My bedroom has changed in the hundred-plus years that passed since I slept there as a child. The floorboards have been carpeted over, torn up, replaced. The walls are thick with new layers of paint. The windows have been upgraded, the closet expanded. The oak tree that stood outside my window is gone, felled by a storm twenty years ago. But the house still stands, and our family still lives here, with all our attendant ghosts. You and I are haunting each other, I think.

I picture you standing in the kitchen downstairs, over a century ago. I imagine that you're staring out through the little window above the sink, your eyes traveling down the path that descends from the back door and splits at the creek; one trail leads to the pond, and the other leads to the shelter and the anachronopede, with its rows of capsules and blinking lights.

Maybe it's the afternoon you left us. June 22, 1963: storm clouds gathering in the west, the wind picking up, the air growing heavy with the threat of rain. You're staring out the window, gazing across the dewy fields at the forking path, trying to decide which one you'll take.

My bedroom is just above the kitchen, and my window has that same view, a little expanded—I can see clear down to the pond where Dad and I used to sit on his weeks off from the oil fields. It's spring, and the cattails are only hip high. I can just make out the silhouette of a great blue heron walking among the reeds and rushes.

You and I, we're twenty feet and more than a hundred years apart.

***

You went into labor not knowing my name, which I know now is unprecedented in our family: you knew Dad's name before you laid eyes on him, the time and date of my birth, the hospital where he would drive you when you went into labor. But my name? My sex? Conspicuously absent on Uncle Dante's gilt-edged book where all these happy details were recorded in advance.

Dad told me later that you thought I'd be a stillbirth. He didn't know about the record book, about the blank space where a name should go. But he told me that nothing he said while you were pregnant could convince you I'd come into the world alive. You thought I'd slip out of you strangled and blue, already decaying.

Instead, I started screaming before they pulled me all the way out.

Dad said that even when the nurse placed me in your arms, you thought you were hallucinating. "I had to tell her, over and over: Miriam, you're not dreaming, our daughter is alive."

I bit my lip when he told me that, locked the words "your son" out of sight. I regret that now; maybe I could have explained myself to him. I should have tried, at least.

You didn't name me for nearly a week.

***

1954 tastes like Kellogg's Rice Krispies in fresh milk, delivered earlier that morning. It smells like woodsmoke, cedar chips, Dad's Camel cigarettes mixed with the perpetual stink of diesel in his clothes. It feels like the worn velvet nap of the couch in our living room, which I loved to run my fingers across.

I was four years old. I woke up in the middle of the night after a loud crash of lightning. The branches of the oak tree outside my window were thrashing in the wind and the rain.

I crept out of bed, dragging my blanket. I slipped out of the door and into the hallway, heading for your and Dad's bedroom. I stopped when I heard voices coming from the parlor downstairs: I recognized your sharp tones, but there was also a man's voice, not Dad's baritone but something closer to a tenor.

The door creaked when I pushed it open, and the voices fell silent. I paused, and then you yanked open the door.

The curlers in your hair had come undone, descending toward your shoulders. I watched one tumble out of your hair and onto the floor like a stunned beetle. I only caught a glimpse of the man standing in the corner; he had thin, hunched shoulders and dark hair, wet and plastered to his skull. He was wearing one of Dad's old robes with the initials monogrammed on the pocket. It was much too big for him.

You snatched me up, not gently, and carried me up to the bedroom you shared with Dad.

"Tom," you hissed. You dropped me on the bed before Dad was

fully awake. He sat up, blinking at me, and looked to you for an explanation.

"There's a visitor," you said, voice strained.

Dad looked at the clock, pulling it closer to him to get a proper look. "Now? Who is it?"

Your jaw was clenched, and so were your hands. "I'm handling it. I just need you to watch—"

You said my name in a way I'd never heard it before, as if each syllable were a hard, steel ball dropping from your lips. It frightened me, and I started to cry. Silently, though, since I didn't want you to notice me. I didn't want you to look at me with eyes like that.

You turned on your heel and left the room, locking the door behind you.

Dad patted me on the back, his wide hand nearly covering the expanse of my skinny shoulders. "It's all right, kid," he said. "Nothing to be scared of. Why don't you lie down and I'll read you something."

In the morning, there was no sign a visitor had been there at all. You and Dad assured me that I must have dreamed the whole thing.

I know now you were lying. I think I knew it even then.

***

I had two childhoods.

One happened between Dad's ten-day hitches in the White County oil fields. That childhood smells like his tobacco, wool coats, wet grass. It sounds like the opening theme songs to all our favorite TV shows. It tastes like the peanut-butter sandwiches you'd pack for us, which we'd eat down by the pond, the same one I can just barely see from my window. In the summer, we'd sit at the edge of the water, dipping our toes into the mud. Sometimes Dad told me stories or asked me to fill him in on the episodes of *Gunsmoke* and *Science Fiction Theater* he'd missed, and we'd chat while watching for birds. The herons have always been my favorite, stepping cautiously through the shallow water. Sometimes, we'd catch sight of one flying overhead, its wide wings fighting against gravity.

And then there was the childhood with you, and with Dara—the childhood that happened when Dad was away. I remember the first morning I came downstairs and she was eating pancakes off of your fancy china, the plates that were decorated with delicate paintings of evening primrose.

"Hi there. I'm Dara," she said.

When I looked at you, shy and unsure, you told me, "She's a cousin. She'll be dropping in when your father is working. Just to keep us company."

Dara didn't look much like you, I thought, not the way that Dad's cousins and uncles all resembled each other. But I could see a few similarities between the two of you—hazel eyes, long fingers, and something I didn't have the words to describe for a long time: a certain discomfort, the sense that you held yourselves slightly apart from the rest of us. It had made you a figure of gossip in town, though I didn't know that until high school, when the same was true of me.

"What should I call you?" Dara asked me.

You jumped in and told her to call me by my name, the one you'd chosen for me, after the week of indecision following my birth. How can I ever make you understand how much I disliked that name? It felt like it belonged to a sister I'd never known, whose legacy I could never fulfill or surpass or even forget. Dara must have caught the face I made, because later, when you were out in the garden, she asked me, "Do you have another name? One you want me to call you instead?"

When I shrugged, she said, "It doesn't have to be a forever name. Just one for the day. You can introduce yourself differently every time you see me."

And so every morning when I woke up and saw Dara sitting at the table, I gave her a different name: Doc, Buck, George, Charlie. The names of my heroes from television and comics and the matinees in town. They weren't my name, but they were better than the one you gave me. I liked the way they sounded, the shape of them rolling around my mouth.

You just looked on, lips pursed in a frown, and told Dara you wished she'd quit indulging my silly little games.

The two of you sat around our kitchen table and—if I was quiet and didn't draw any attention to myself—talked in a strange code about *jumps* and *fastenings* and *capsules,* dropping the names of people I never knew. More of your cousins, I figured.

You told the neighbors that all of your family was spread out and disinclined to make the long trip to visit. When Dara took me in, she made up a tale about a long-lost cousin whose parents had kicked him out for being trans. Funny the way the truth seeps into lies.

***

I went to see Uncle Dante in 1927. I wanted to see what he had in that book of his about me, and about you and Dara.

1927 tastes like the chicken broth and brown bread he fed me after I showed up at his door. It smells like the musty blanket he hung around my shoulders, like kerosene lamps and cigar smoke. It sounds like the scratchy records he played on his phonograph: Duke Ellington and Al Jolson, the Gershwin brothers and Gene Austin.

"Your mother dropped in back in '24," he said, settling down in an armchair in front of the fireplace. It was the same fireplace that had been in our parlor, though Dad had sealed off the chimney in 1958, saying it let in too many drafts. "She was very adamant that your name be written down in the records. She seemed…upset." He let the last word hang on its own, lonely, obviously understated.

"That's not my name," I told him. "It's the one she gave me, but it was never mine."

I had to explain to him then—he'd been to the future, and so it didn't seem so farfetched, my transition. I simplified it for him, didn't go into HRT or mastectomies, the phalloplasty I'd scheduled a century and a half in the future. I skipped the introduction to gender theory, Susan Stryker, *Stone Butch Blues*, all the things Dara gave me to read when I asked for books about people like me.

"My aunt Lucia was of a similar disposition," Uncle Dante told me. "Once her last child was grown, she gave up on dresses entirely. Wore a suit to church for her last twelve years, which gave her a reputation for eccentricity."

I clamped my mouth shut and nodded, still feeling ill and shaky from the jump. The smell of his cigar burned in my nostrils. I wished we could have had the conversation outside, on the porch; the parlor seemed too familiar, too laden with the ghost of your presence.

"What name should I put instead?" he asked, pulling the gilt-edged journal down from the mantle.

"It's blank when I'm born," I told him. He paused in the act of sharpening his pencil; he knew better than to write the future in ink. "Just erase it. White it out if you need to."

He sat back in his chair, and combed his fingers through his beard. "That's unprecedented."

"Not anymore," I said.

*   *   *

1963 feels like a menstrual cramp, like the ache in my legs as my bones stretched, like the twinges in my nipples as my breasts developed. It smells like Secret roll-on deodorant and the menthol cigarettes you had taken up smoking. It tastes like the peach cobbler I burned in Home Ec class, which the teacher forced me to eat. It sounds like Sam Cooke's album *Night Beat*, which Dara, during one of her visits, told me to buy.

And it looks like you, jumpier than I'd ever seen you, so twitchy that even Dad commented on it before he left for his hitch in the oil fields.

"Will you be all right?" he asked after dinner.

I was listening to the two of you talk from the kitchen doorway. I'd come in to ask Dad if he was going to watch *Gunsmoke* with me and caught the two of you with your heads together.

You leaned forward, bracing your hands on the edge of the sink, looking as if you couldn't hold yourself up, as if gravity was working just a little bit harder on you than it was on everyone else. I wondered for a second if you were going to tell him about Dara. I'd grown up keeping her a secret with you, though the omission had begun to weigh heavy on me. I loved Dad, and I loved Dara; being unable to reconcile the two of them seemed trickier each passing week.

Instead you said nothing. You relaxed your shoulders, and you smiled for him and kissed his cheek. You said the two of us would be fine, not to worry about his girls.

The very next day, you pulled me out of bed and showed me our family's time machine, in the old tornado shelter with the lock I'd never been able to pick.

***

I know more about the machine now, after talking with Uncle Dante, reading the records. The mysterious man, Moses Stone, built it in 1905, when Grandma Emmeline's parents leased out a parcel of land. He called it the anachronopede, which probably sounded marvelous in 1905, but even Uncle Dante was rolling his eyes at the name twenty years later. I know that Stone took Emmeline on trips to the future when she was seventeen, and then abandoned her after a few years, and nobody's been able to find him since then. I know that the machine is keyed to something in Emmeline's matrilineal DNA, some recessive gene.

I wonder if Stone built the anachronopede as an experiment. An experiment needs parameters, right? So build a machine that only certain people in one family can use. We can't go back before 1905, when the machine was completed, and we can't go past August 3, 2321. What happens that day? The only way to find out is to go as far forward as possible, and then wait. Maroon yourself in time. Exile yourself in the future, where none of us can reach you.

I'm sure you were lonely, waiting for me to grow up so you could travel again. You were exiled when you married Dad in 1947, in that feverish period just after the war. It must have been so romantic at first. I've seen the letters he wrote during the years he courted you. You'd grown up seeing his name written next to yours, with the date that you'd marry him. When did you start feeling trapped, I wonder? You were caught in a weird net of fate and love and the future and the past. You loved Dad, but your love kept you hostage. You loved me, but you knew that someday I'd transform myself into someone you didn't recognize.

***

At first, when you took me underground to see the anachronopede, I thought you and Dad had built a fallout shelter. But there were no beds or boxes of canned food. Built into the rocky wall were rows of doors that looked like the one on our icebox. Round light bulbs were installed above the doors, nearly all of them red, though one or two were slowly blinking between orange and yellow.

All the doors were shut except for two, near the end, which hung ajar.

"Those two capsules are for us, you and me," you said. "Nobody else can use them."

I stared at them. "What are they for?"

I'd heard you and Dara speak in code for nearly all of my life—*jumps* and *capsules* and *fastenings*. I'd imagined all sorts of things. Aliens and spaceships and doorways to another dimension, all the things I'd seen Truman Bradley introduce on *Science Fiction Theater*.

"Traveling," you said.

"In time or in space?"

You seemed surprised. I'm not sure why. Dad collected pulp magazines, and you'd given me books by H.G. Wells and Jules Verne for Christmas. The Justice League had gone into the future. I'd seen *The Fly* during a half-price matinee. You know how it was back then: such things weren't considered impossible so much as inevitable. The future was a country we all wanted so badly to visit.

"In time," you said.

I immediately started peppering you with questions: how far into the future had you gone? When were you born? Had you seen dinosaurs? Had you met King Arthur? What about jetpacks? Was Dara from the future?

You held a hand to your mouth, watching as I danced around the small cavern, firing off questions like bullets sprayed from a Tommy gun.

"Maybe you are too young," you said, staring at the two empty capsules in the wall.

"I'm not!" I insisted. "Can't we go somewhere? Just a quick jump?"

I added the last part because I wanted you to know I'd been listening, when you and Dara had talked in code at the kitchen table. I'd been waiting for you include me in the conversation.

"Tomorrow," you decided. "We'll leave tomorrow."

***

The first thing I learned about time travel was that you couldn't eat anything before you did it. And you could only take a few sips of water: no juice or milk. The second thing I learned was that it was the most painful thing in the world, at least for me.

"Your grandmother Emmeline called it the fastening," you told me. "She said it felt like being a button squeezed through a too-narrow slit in a piece of fabric. It affects everyone differently."

"How's it affect you?"

You twisted your wedding ring around on your finger. "I haven't done it since before you were born."

You made me go to the bathroom twice before we walked that path, taking the fork that led to the shelter. The grass was still wet with dew, and there was a chill in the air. Up above, thin wispy clouds were scratched onto the sky, but out west, I could see dark clouds gathering. There'd be storms later.

But what did I care about later? I was going into a time machine.

I asked you, "Where are we going?"

You replied, "To visit Dara. Just a quick trip."

There was something cold in your voice. I recognized the tone, the same you used when trying to talk me into wearing the new dress you'd bought me for church, or telling me to stop tearing through the house and play quietly for once.

In the shelter, you helped me undress, though it made me feel hotly embarrassed and strange to be naked in front of you. I'd grown wary of my own body in the last few months, the way it was changing: I'd been dismayed by the way my nipples had grown tender, at the fatty flesh that budded beneath them. It seemed like a betrayal.

I hunched my shoulders and covered my privates, though you barely glanced at my naked skin. You helped me lie down in the capsule, showed me how to pull the round mask over my nose and mouth, attach the clip that went over my index finger. Finally, you lifted one of my arms up and wrapped a black cuff around the crook of my elbow. I noticed, watching you, that you had bitten all of your nails down to the quick, and the edges were jagged and tender-looking.

"You program your destination date in here, you see?" You tapped a square of black glass on the ceiling of the capsule, and it lit up at the touch. Your fingers flew across the screen, typing directly onto it, rearranging colored orbs that seemed to attach themselves to your finger.

"You'll learn how to do this on your own eventually," you said. The screen, accepting whatever you'd done to it, blinked out and went black again.

I breathed through my mask. A whisper of air blew against my skin, a rubbery, stale, lemony scent.

"Don't be scared," you said. "I'll be there when you wake up. I'm sending myself back a little earlier, so I'll be there to help you out of the capsule."

You kissed me on the forehead and shut the door. I was left alone in the dark as the walls around me started to hum.

Calling it "the fastening" does it a disservice. It's much more painful than that. Granny Emmeline is tougher than I'll ever be, if she thought it was just like forcing a button into place.

For me, it felt like being crushed in a vise lined with broken glass and nails. I understood, afterward, why you had forbidden me from eating or drinking for twenty-four hours. I would have vomited in the mask, shat myself inside the capsule. I came back to myself in the dark, wild with terror and the phantom sensations of that awful pain.

The door opened. The light needled into my eyes, and I screamed, trying to cover them.

Hands reached in and pushed me down, and eventually, I registered your voice in my ear, though not what you were saying. I stopped flailing long enough for all the straps and cuffs to be undone, and then I was pulled out of the capsule. You held me in your arms, rocking and soothing me, rubbing my back as I cried hysterically onto your shoulder.

When my sobs died away to hiccups, I realized that we weren't alone in the shelter. Dara was with us as well, and she had thrown a blanket over my shoulders.

"Jesus, Miriam," she said, over and over. "What the hell were you thinking?"

I found out later that I was the youngest person in my family to ever make a jump. Traditionally, they made their first jumps on their seventeenth birthday. I was nearly five years shy.

You smoothed back a lock of my hair, and I saw that all your fingernails had lost their ragged edges. Instead, they were rounded and smooth, topped with little crescents of white.

***

Uncle Dante told me it wasn't unusual for two members of the family to be lovers, especially if there were generational gaps between them. It helped to avoid romantic entanglements with people who were bound to linear lives, at least until one of us was ready to settle down for a number of years and raise children. Pregnancy didn't mix well with time travel. It was odder to do what you had done: settle down with someone who was, as Dara liked to put it, stuck in the slow lane of linear time.

Dara told me about the two of you, eventually; that you'd been lovers before you met Dad, before you settled down with him in 1947. And that when she started visiting us in 1955, she wasn't sleeping alone in the guest bedroom.

I'm not sure if I was madder at her or you at the time, though I've since forgiven her. Why wouldn't I? You've left both of us, and it's a big thing, to have that in common.

***

1981 is colored silver, beige, bright orange, deep brown. It feels like the afghan blanket Dara kept on my bed while I recovered from my first jump, some kind of cheap fake wool. It tastes like chicken soup and weak tea with honey and lime Jell-O.

And for a few days, at least, 1981 felt like a low-grade headache that never went away, muscle spasms that I couldn't always control, dry mouth, difficulty swallowing. It smelt like a lingering olfactory hallucination of frying onions. It sounded like a ringing in my ears.

"So you're the unnamed baby, huh?" Dara said, that first morning when I woke up. She was reading a book, and she set it down next to her on the couch.

I was disoriented: you and Dara had placed me in the southeast bedroom, the same one I slept in all through my childhood. (The same one I'm recovering in right now.) I'm not sure if you thought it would comfort me, to wake up to familiar surroundings. It was profoundly strange, to be in my own bedroom but have it be so different: the striped wallpaper replaced with avocado green paint; a loveseat with floral upholstering where my dresser had been; all my posters of Buck Rogers and Superman replaced with framed paintings of unfamiliar artwork.

"Dara?" I said. She seemed different, colder. Her hair was shorter than the last time I'd seen her, and she wore a pair of thick-framed glasses.

She cocked her head. "That'd be me. Nice to meet you."

I blinked at her, still disoriented and foggy. "We met before," I said.

She raised her eyebrows, like she couldn't believe I was so dumb. "Not by my timeline."

Right. Time travel.

You rushed in then. You must have heard us talking. You crouched down next to me and stroked the hair back from my face.

"How are you feeling?" you asked.

I looked down at your fingernails, and saw again that they were smooth, with a hint of white at the edges. Dara told me later that you'd arrived two days before me, just so you two could have some time to be together. After all, the two of you had parted ways only a few weeks before, by Dara's timeline. You had some catching up to do.

"All right, I guess," I told you.

***

Those first few days, it felt like the worst family vacation. Dara was distant with me and downright cold to you. I caught snippets of the arguments you had with Dara—always whispered in doorways, or downstairs in the kitchen, the words too faint for me to make out.

It got a little better once I was back on my feet, able to walk around and explore. I was astonished by everything: the walnut trees on our property that I had known as saplings now towered over me. Dara's television was twice the size of ours, in color, and had over a dozen stations. Dara's car seemed tiny and shaped like a snake's head, instead of the generous curves and lines of the cars I knew.

I think it charmed Dara out of her anger a bit, to see me so appreciative of all these futuristic wonders—which were all relics of the past for her—and the conversations between the three of us got a little bit easier. Dara told me a little bit more about where she'd come from—the late twenty-first century—and why she was in this time—studying with some poet I'd never heard of. She showed me the woman's poetry, and though I couldn't make much of it out at the time, one line has always stuck with me. "I did not recognize the shape of my own name."

I pondered that, lying awake in my bedroom, the once and future bedroom that I'm writing this from now, that I slept in then, that I awoke in when I was a young child, frightened by a storm.

The rest of that poem made little sense to me, but I know about names, and hearing the one that's been given to you, and not recognizing it. I was trying to stammer this out to Dara one night, after she'd read that poem to me. And she asked, plain as could be, "What would you rather be called instead?"

I thought about how I used to introduce myself like the heroes of the TV shows my father and I watched: Doc and George and Charlie. It had been a silly game, but there'd been something more serious underneath it. I'd recognized something in the shape of those names, something I wanted for myself.

"I dunno. A boy's name," I said. "Like George in the Famous Five."

"Well, why do you want to be called by a boy's name?" Dara asked gently.

In the corner, where you'd been playing solitaire, you paused while laying down a card. Dara noticed too, and we both looked over at you. I cringed, wondering what you were about to say; you hated that I didn't like my name.

But you said nothing, just resumed playing, slapping the cards down a little more heavily than before.

∗∗∗

I forgive you for drugging me to take me back to 1963. I know I screamed at you after we arrived and the drugs wore off, but I was also a little relieved. It was a sneaking sort of relief, and didn't do much to counterbalance the feelings of betrayal and rage, but I know I would have panicked the second you shoved me into one of those capsules.

You'd taken me to the future, after all. I'd seen the relative wonders of 1981: VHS tapes, the Flash Gordon movie, the Columbia

Space Shuttle. I would have forgiven you so much for that tiny glimpse.

I don't forgive you for leaving me, though. I don't forgive you for the morning after, when I woke up in my old familiar bedroom and padded downstairs for a bowl of cereal and found, instead, a note that bore two words in your handwriting: *I'm sorry.*

The note rested atop the gilt-edged book that Grandma Emmeline had started as a diary, and that Uncle Dante had turned into both a record and a set of instructions for future generations: the names, birthdates, and locations for all the traveling members of our family; who lived in the house and when; and sometimes, how and when a person died. The book stays with the house; you must have kept it hidden in the attic.

I flipped through it until I found your name: Miriam Guthrie (nee Stone): born November 21, 1977, Harrisburg, IL. Next to it, you penciled in the following.

Jumped forward to June 22, 2321 CE, and will die in exile beyond reach of the anachronopede.

Two small words could never encompass everything you have to apologize for.

***

I wonder if you ever looked up Dad's obituary. I wonder if you were even able to, if the record for one small man's death even lasts that long.

When you left, you took my father's future with you. He was stuck in the slow lane of linear time, and for Dad, the future he'd dreamed of must have receded into the distance, something he'd never be able to reach.

He lost his job in the fall of 1966, as the White County oil wells ran dry, and hanged himself in the garage six months later. Dara cut him down and called the ambulance. Her visits became more regular after you left us. She must have known the day he would die.

(I can't bring myself to ask her: couldn't she have arrived twenty minutes earlier and stopped him? I don't want to know her answer.)

In that obituary, I'm first in the list of those who survived him, and it's the last time I used the name you gave me. During the funeral, I nodded, received hugs and handshakes from Dad's cousins and friends, bowed my head when the priest instructed, prayed hard for his soul. When it was done, I walked alone to the pond where the two of us had sat together, watching birds and talking about the plots of silly television shows. I tried to remember everything that I could about him, trying to preserve his ghost against the vagaries of time: the smell of Camel cigarettes and diesel on his clothes, the red-blond stubble that dotted his jaw, the way his eyes brightened when they landed on you.

I wished so hard that you were there with me. I wanted to cry on your shoulder, to sob as hard and hysterically as I had when you took me to 1981. I wanted to be able to slap you, hit you, to push you in the water and hold you beneath the surface. I could have killed you that day.

When I was finished, Dara took me back to the house. We cleaned it as best we could for the next family member who would live here. There always has to be a member of the Stone family here, to take care of the shelter, the anachronopede, and the travelers who come through.

Then she took me away, to 2073, the home she'd made more than a century away from you.

***

Today was the first day I was able to leave the house, to take cautious, wobbling steps to the outside world. Everything is still tender and bruised, though my body is healing faster than I ever thought possible. It feels strange to walk with a weight between my legs; I walk differently, with a wider stride, even though I'm still limping.

Dara and I walked down to the pond today. The frogs all hushed at our approach, but the blackbirds set up a racket. And off in the distance, a heron lifted a cautious foot and placed it down again. Its beak darted into the water and came back up with a wriggling fish, which it flipped into its mouth. I suppose it was satisfied with that, because it crouched down, spread its wings, and then jumped into the air, enormous wings fighting against gravity until it rose over the trees.

Three days before my surgery, I went back to you. The pain of it is always the same, like I'm being torn apart and placed back together with clumsy, inexpert fingers, but by now I've gotten used to it. I wanted you to see me as the man I've always known I am, the man I slowly became. And I wanted to see if I could forgive you—if I could look at you and see anything besides my father's slow decay, my own broken and betrayed heart.

I knocked at the door, dizzy, ears ringing, shivering, soaked from the storm that was so much worse than I remembered. I was lucky that you or Dara had left a blanket in the shelter so I didn't have to walk up to the front door naked, my flat, scarred chest at odds with my wide hips, the thatch of pubic hair with no flesh protruding from it. I'd been on hormones for a year, and this second puberty reminded me so much of my first one, with you in 1963: the acne and the awkwardness, the slow reveal of my future self.

You answered the door with your hair in curlers, just as I remembered, and fetched me one of Dad's old robes. I fingered the monogramming at the breast pocket, and I wished, so hard, that I could walk upstairs and see him.

"What the hell," you said. "I thought the whole family knew these years were off limits while I'm linear."

You didn't quite recognize me, and you tilted your head.

"Have we met before?"

I looked you in the eye, and my voice cracked when I told you I was your son.

Your hand went to your mouth. "I'll have a son?" you asked.

And I told you the truth: "You have one already."

Your hand went to your gut, as if you would be sick. You shook your head so hard that your curlers started coming loose. That's when the door creaked open, just a crack. You flew over there and yanked it all the way open, snatching the child up in your arms. I barely caught a glimpse of my own face looking back at me as you carried my child-self up the stairs.

I left before I could introduce myself to you. My name is Heron, Mama. I haven't forgiven you yet, but maybe someday I will. And when I do, I will travel back one last time, to that night you left me and Dad for the future. I'll tell you that your apology has finally been accepted, and I will give you my blessing to live in exile, marooned in a future beyond all reach.

NOT AN OCEAN, BUT THE SEA

Nadia found the ocean behind the Swedish assholes' couch during her weekly cleaning. She had followed a small trail of sand to the eastern wall with the vacuum, and when she'd moved the couch to vacuum underneath it, there was the ocean, snuggled right up to the wall. A fresh wind blew off it, stirring the curtains: the smell of salt and mud.

The Swedish assholes' stupid cat jumped up on the couch and stared down at the ocean like he could see beneath the surface: the fish, the plankton, the sharks and all. His tail twitched.

Nadia had dubbed these particular clients "the Swedish assholes" for many reasons, most prominently because they insisted she use their vacuum. Their vacuum was an awful, rattling hunk of junk with a hose that connected directly to air vents installed in the walls of their high-rise. It was nearly impossible to reach all the floors with it. But they'd had it mail-ordered from a Swedish design company and insisted it was better than hers, which had been purchased from a cousin's appliance store and was kept in perfect working order.

The ocean behind the couch, she thought, had probably not been ordered from IKEA or Electrolux.

Nadia cleaned houses because the money was decent and she could do it alone. She was forty-eight, Ukrainian, had never been very beautiful, and had outlived most of her family. Sometimes she stole the loose coins from the bedrooms she cleaned, not for the money but for the thrill. She was not a woman given to romance or fancy, but sometimes thought she should have been the witch in a fairytale, alone in the forest except when she wanted to make mischief for men. If she was honest, though, she lacked the imagination to be a witch. Mischief didn't come naturally to her.

"Shoo," Nadia said to the cat. He bent his ears back and glared and didn't move until she waved the vacuum's upholstery attachment at him. Nadia moved the couch back into place and continued vacuuming. There was much left to clean in the Swedish assholes' apartment. She hadn't even started on the kitchen, where the many chrome gadgets were always splattered with sauces. God save her from rich people who thought they knew how to cook.

Nadia mostly forgot about the incident until the next week, when she again had to move the couch to vacuum. It always caught her off guard. Nadia would see the sand first, then catch the smell, and remember: of course, the Swedish assholes had an ocean under their couch.

The day that changed was not very different from the preceding ones. Not unseasonably cold, nor warm. Nadia was still divorced, childless, an immigrant who lived in an enclave of other immigrants, who understood the true value of things.

Had she slept poorly the night before? Nadia rarely slept well, with vivid dreams that routinely woke her before dawn. Was her back bothering her that day? Yes, but not as much as her knees; her knees were her real problem. All that time spent scrubbing floors, all kinds of floors, tile and linoleum and bamboo and one man who had furnished his children's playroom with a floor made of pennies. It was ghastly, a nightmare to clean, and she had Abraham Lincoln's face permanently embedded in her knees now.

On that day, Nadia arrived at the Swedish assholes' apartment at her normal time. Nadia dropped her purse, then her bucket of cleaning supplies, and then her coat. The stupid cat watched her from the kitchen counter where he was surely forbidden to sit, and she watched him back. Then she strode into the living room, hauled the couch away from the eastern wall, and stared down at the small ocean that hid beneath it.

It looked like the Black Sea, she decided. Not the sea of her memories, with its dirty-colored sand and leathery old men leering at bikini-clad girls, but the sea of her dreams, with dark water that contained shipwrecks and other unknowable things.

Nadia shed her clothes, placing them on the back of the couch: the old, stained jeans; the cheap and scratchy T-shirt emblazoned with the name of the cleaning company; her threadbare bra; her soft panties with the torn lace at the hem. Then she stood at the lip of the sea, of *her* sea, and dipped in a toe. She knew that the best way to get into cold water was not to hesitate, not to shriek and fumble, but to steadily allow oneself to be submerged.

Rather than letting her sink in, however, the sea rose to meet Nadia, spilling out over the stingy inch of sand that formed its beach, lazily spreading across the floor of the Swedish assholes' fourteenth-floor apartment. It quickly submerged the mohair rugs and the lower bookshelves, the white lacquer coffee table littered with fashion and design magazines. It rose higher than the air vents of the designer vacuum, until salty water began leaking down the pipes. Wavelets lapped against the cream-colored walls.

The Swedish assholes' stupid cat leapt up onto the couch, perching on Nadia's clothes. He watched the water with fascination, but no real concern. He raised a paw as if to swat at something under the surface, then brought it to his mouth and licked it instead, as if that was what he had meant to do all along.

PRESQUE VU

Five rides, Clay told himself after he gagged up that morning's haunting. He'd pick up five rides today, and then he'd call it quits.

He'd woken up choking on house keys nearly every morning for the last two months, a curious sort of morning sickness. Today's was brass with a hexagonal head, old and scratched. Clay caught the haunting before it fell into the toilet, warm from his body and sticky with mucus. He washed his hands and the key, dried them, and then dropped the key into the jar he kept in the bathroom. It was nearly full; he'd have to get a larger one soon.

Five rides and no more. He'd do them during the day and be home before dark.

He thought of his last passenger the night before. Halloween had ended weeks ago, but people in town still wore cheap masks and polyester and satin costumes, more of them out on the streets every night. She'd been dressed in a brown onesie, with a plastic monkey mask too small for her face.

"It's Halloween *every* day," she'd slurred as her friends poured her into his backseat. "There are ghosts everywhere, see?"

She pointed out the window at one of the wraiths twisted up in black scraps of fabric, bleeding purple light from its eyes, mouths, and fingertips. The wraiths dotted the street, wandering in and out of traffic and bars, standing sentry atop bus shelters.

"I hate them," the girl said petulantly, leaning her head against the window. The plastic mask squeaked against the glass. "They're awful, the way they stare at you." He'd left her on the curb after she demanded he pull over so she could puke.

Clay pulled on a hoodie and a pair of jeans before stumbling to the apartment below his. Mari, in 2B, was infinitely generous with her cheap coffee, and she was sometimes his only human contact outside of driving for Flock.

Clay could hear calm music and a British voice on the other side of the door, probably one of the nature documentaries she watched ceaselessly. He knocked loudly. When she opened the door, strains of oboes and violins washed over him, along with the smell of Mari's apartment: sage and weed smoke, lavender, sautéed onions.

"Coffee?" she asked, speaking over the TV.

Mari's living room was crowded with shabby furniture and mismatched pillows, potted plants and unfinished craft projects. Clay's apartment contained his bed, a table with two mismatched chairs, and piles of clothes in varying states of cleanliness.

Mari had the coffee things out, the big yellow can of Bustelo and an aeropress. The little TV in the corner of the kitchen was showing clips of crows, and the noise of their cawing filled the apartment. They circled through gray skies and perched on telephone wires, calling to each other. They remembered people's faces, the narrator said. They remembered what people had done to them for generations.

"So, Clay." Mari didn't seem to mind that she had to shout over the TV. "You're queer, right?"

Mari had a briefcase full of sex toys with a Bisexual Pride bumper sticker on the front. He knew this because she had pointed it out in the living room and said, "That's where I keep my sex toys. Most of them, anyway."

Clay blinked and said, "Why?"

"What?"

"I said—" His throat flared with pain, and he gestured for her to turn the sound down on the TV. When she did, he said, "Why do you want to know?"

"I wanted to ask you a favor, but I didn't want to presume. I kind of *figured* you were, because of that conversation about Terry Crews—"

"I don't know anyone who wouldn't want to get lovingly crushed between his thighs," he said, an automatic reaction. "But yeah. Confirmed queer."

"Cool. So Finn wants me to peg him, but he wants to know what bottoming is like from someone with a prostate. And I'm not presuming anything about *your* tastes and preferences, but…Your look of horror is pretty cute, for the record."

"Thanks." Clay ran a hand over his face. He had not been prepared for that conversational turn. He wasn't sure he would ever be prepared for it. "I'm not sure I can talk to you about anal sex when I'm barely awake."

"You don't need to talk to *me* about it. I want you to talk to Finn."

Finn was Mari's boyfriend, and not that it was Clay's business, but she could do better. The first and only time he'd met Finn, the other man pressured Clay to drink nettle tea and read Pema Chödrön, "To help keep your life in balance." Mari, meanwhile, worked at a suicide hotline, spoke English, Tagolog, Mandarin, and Spanish, and freely shared her weed and bad coffee. Clay knew which of these things helped keep him balanced.

"Is there a reason Finn can't just google *how to take it up the butt*?" Clay said.

"It's *Finn*. He wants locally sourced advice about anal pleasure."
Mari plunked a cup of coffee in front of him. "I'll cut your hair in
exchange. And make you dinner tonight. I have people coming over
anyway."

"What's wrong with my hair?"

"When's the last time you cut it?"

Clay couldn't remember. Things had been too hectic, too weird
before he'd left the city; things had been too lonely and weird since
he'd arrived.

"I'll even set you up on a date," Mari offered. "There's a cute
intern at the hotline."

"I'm not fucking an intern," Clay said, though he wasn't sure
why he objected.

"At least let me cut your hair. It's starting to look like a hockey
mullet."

Mari had her own inertia, and Clay soon found himself on her
balcony, looking out at the abandoned construction project in the
fields beyond their backyard. Billboards along the road still advertised
new homes, built to order. But the project had stalled. None of the
homes were built, and all that remained were enormous gouges in the
ground where they'd dug foundations. A couple wraiths lingered by
the edges, little blurs of black and purple gazing down into the pits.

Clay sat on a milk carton while Mari moved around him, comb-
ing through his hair with her fingers and snipping with a confidence
that relaxed him. She pitched his hair into the wind. He thought
about birds building their nests with it.

"What's Finn haunted by?" he asked.

The movement of Mari's fingers slowed. "Unspooled cassette
tapes. He wakes up with the tape knotted in his hair."

"What type of music?" Clay asked.

"We don't listen to them," Mari said. "I get postcards."

Clay had seen Mari's hauntings, since all of their mail was mixed together. The postcards were vintage, with terrible puns and bland innuendo: the one he'd seen had a naughty librarian with stacks of books propping up her cleavage, and beneath it the words *Interested in a thriller?* On the other side was a spidery scrawl in faded brown ink. He'd slipped it under her door without reading it and washed his hands after. It felt terrible to touch someone else's haunting.

"Mine are house keys," Clay said. "I wake up with them stuck in my throat."

"Do they unlock things?"

"I don't know. I haven't tried."

Mari fished a pair of clippers out of her bag and plugged them in. Clay shivered as she touched them to his scalp.

"Cool," she said a moment later, tilting his head up. "You look slightly less like you're about to murder a cabin full of teenagers."

Clay shook his head, marveling at how light it felt. "Thanks."

"So?"

"I'll talk to Finn about taking it up the ass. Although I don't know when—"

Mari waved a hand. "I'll set it up. It's not a pegging emergency; you can take a couple days."

***

Clay's phone pinged as he was pulling out of the parking lot: a ride request just a hundred feet down the road, from a user named Natasha. She'd uploaded a picture of herself, an olive-skinned woman with long brown hair, smiling in nostalgic, filtered light.

Clay saw a figure by the abandoned construction site, perched at the edge of an unfinished foundation. Was it a wraith? Clay had picked up wraiths before, though he worried about being seen with one in his car. The wraiths weren't bad customers. They tipped. They were never drunk or obnoxious. And they didn't talk, though some of them sang in low, mournful voices. If Clay wasn't in the mood to listen, he just turned the radio up. They were easily drowned out, unlike some of his living passengers.

Clay pulled over, rolled down the window, and called out, "Natasha? Going to the Riverside apartments?"

The figure waved, though Clay wasn't sure if it was in affirmation or negation. As she came closer, Clay realized she was human, not wraith. She had a hat pulled down to the rim of her sunglasses, a scarf wrapped up to her nose, and an overlarge jean jacket that draped over her hands. A few strands of brittle black hair stuck out. She limped up to his rear door, opened it, and carefully folded herself into the backseat.

"Natasha?" he asked again. "Riverside apartments?"

"Yeah." A hoarse voice: it sounded like fabric being torn.

"All right." He hit ON ROUTE on the app and started driving.

She had brought the smell of the outdoors with her, rotting leaves and salt and mud, and her presence seemed to fill his car. He didn't dare turn on the radio—it would have felt like listening to music on the way to a funeral—so the silence lay heavy. It was just her labored breathing and the engine, which seemed too soft in comparison.

"Do you live around there?" he asked. "Near the construction site?" Natasha shook her head.

"What were you doing out there?" What he wanted to know was what she'd been doing so close to his house.

"Looking," Natasha said.

"For what?" Clay asked, then realized he might not want to know. "Sorry you didn't find it, whatever it was."

They drove again in silence. The houses and subdivisions, like his and Mari's building, gradually gave way to apartment complexes, Wal-marts, and Targets.

"Do you really want to know what I was trying to find?" Natasha asked.

"No. Not really. That's fine," Clay said. He pressed down a little bit harder on the accelerator. He was going to count this as two rides, he decided. Two of the five he'd allotted himself today.

They passed into the quaint neighborhoods nearer the center of town, old houses with wide front porches interspersed with newer, uglier condos. They were almost at the Riverside apartments when Clay caught movement out of the corner of his eye: Natasha leaning forward, swaying closer to him. The car swerved in the road.

"My skin," she said in her harsh whisper. "They took my skin. It's always so cold now."

"Sorry," he said, and turned up the heat in the car. Both of these, he knew, were meaningless gestures.

"Why?" she asked. "They took something from you, too. I can tell."

Natasha leaned back, and Clay let himself breathe.

They had stopped at a light, only a few blocks from Riverside, when the door opened. Clay twisted around to see Natasha step out of his car, adjust her sunglasses, and shut the door softly behind her. She limped past two lanes of honking cars to the sidewalk, and then turned and started walking in the opposite direction. Clay put the car in park and was about to unbuckle his seatbelt, full of vague thoughts of chasing after her, when his phone pinged.

Natasha had marked the ride complete.

Natasha had tipped him six dollars on a ten-dollar ride.

The light ahead turned green, and the cars in front of Clay started to move. Clay followed. She'd marked the ride complete. That meant she didn't need his help—or at least, didn't particularly want it.

***

Clay turned down a ride request to the airport, and another that originated from one of the frat houses. He killed time by the downtown strip of cafés and brunch spots, waiting for the lunch rush to get out, by trying to imagine what he would tell Finn about getting fucked. Bottoming, that sounded better—specific but not graphic, less likely to trigger the ass-related anxiety that seemed to be the resting state of most hetero guys.

He texted Mari: *What exactly have you done to Finn's ass before now?*

The answer came immediately. *Exactly??* A winking smiling face followed. Mari was fluent in emoji.

God no, just generally, Clay replied.

Peach emoji, pointer finger. *Some touching, not much penetration. He's butt shy.*

If he was butt shy, why did he want to get pegged? Maybe he wanted to prove he was secure enough in his heterosexuality that he could unclench his sphincter and let his hot girlfriend fuck him? Who knew why straight people did anything, really.

There had been a period where Clay had been using the Flock app for hookups. He hadn't meant to, but one day, he'd met the eyes of a passenger in his rearview mirror, and the man had said, "You've got a nice mouth, anyone ever tell you that?" A terrible line, but it did the trick. The weather had still been warm then: bad ideas seemed worth exploring, consequences minimal. The town had shut down its only gay bar a few weeks before Clay arrived—legal troubles, supposedly. Mari had said, "Oh yeah, the city was *really concerned* about underage drinking. That's why they shut down a single bar mostly patronized by old men and married lesbians."

Clay had pulled into a parking lot, and they'd fooled around in the shadow of a pickup truck with a confederate flag sticker on it. The act was defiant enough to make the otherwise mediocre sex hot.

He'd stopped after letting a guy take him home and fuck him. That guy had done it like a porn star, like it was a performance for an audience Clay couldn't see and wasn't included in. Seven different positions over the course of an hour, a stream of filthy invectives in Clay's ear; this was a hero's journey, but Clay was just the mountain being climbed. The guy cried after he came, and that wouldn't have bothered Clay, except the tears, too, felt like performance, like pageantry.

He'd noticed the framed pictures on his way out the door: the guy dressed up in a suit, shaking the hands of other men in suits. One of them looked like the governor that everyone hated, who'd still managed to get re-elected.

That had been the end of hooking up with his passengers. He hadn't had sex since.

He imagined relating this story to Finn, and the other man's delicate look of distaste—or worse, fascination—as Clay described how sex sometimes left him feeling hollow and more alone than if he'd just jerked off in his room to porn gifs on Reddit. Isolation was easier. Keep your eyes on the road and your thoughts to yourself. Don't look back. Don't think about what came before, what was lost, who was gone, who had disappeared. Don't wonder what doors the keys unlocked; don't ask why they haunted you out of everyone in the world.

***

His second ride that day was two middle-aged men. He nearly didn't pick them up: one was dressed in an ill-fitting cop costume, with a fake handlebar mustache and aviator sunglasses. But the other, dressed normally, had spotted the winged Flock decal in Clay's rear window and waved him down.

"Nineteenth and Stein," the normally dressed one said to Clay.

"Got it," Clay said. Short ride, just a couple miles. He could do this.

"I'm telling you, man, it's awesome," the dress-up cop said as they got in.

"I don't care. You look like one of the faggots from the YMCA song."

Clay hadn't heard anyone use the word "faggot" since he'd ditched his hometown, ten years before. The sound of it now made something in his chest buckle, like it was in danger of collapsing. Keep driving, he told himself, even as his skin prickled.

"Young man! There's no need to feel down!" the cop sang. His voice boomed in the confines of the car.

"Would you shut up? Let the guy fucking drive us in peace."

They turned down Magritte Avenue. The normally dressed guy tried to catch Clay's gaze in the rearview mirror, in silent apology perhaps, but Clay kept his eyes forward.

"You ever unwind one of them?" the dress-up cop asked. He tapped a finger against the window. A wraith was hunched over in a bus shelter, its hands resting on the sidewalk in puddles of violet light. "The purple stuff goes everywhere. Splashes up your arms like blood, stinks like sulfur. It dries, but you'll smell it on your skin through a couple showers."

"No wonder you fucking stink," the other guy said. Clay had noticed it too: the man smelled like someone had lit a match and set fire to a pile of dirty clothes.

"It keeps the hauntings away," the dress-up cop said.

The other guy rolled his eyes, mostly for Clay's benefit. "Nobody really believes that."

"I haven't found any game pieces in my shoes for a week." The cop looked at Clay. "You know they're connected, right? They have to be."

Clay shrugged noncommittally. The man leaned forward, and the smell of sulfur thickened in the car. "You even speak English? I haven't heard a damn word from you yet. What's your name, any-way?"

"I speak English," Clay said. "And I don't know anything about the hauntings."

The other guy pulled the cop back against his seat. "That's enough, man, he's gonna crash if you don't leave him the fuck *alone*."

The cop settled down, softly singing "YMCA" to himself. Clay let the two men off at Nineteenth and Stein. The dress-up cop got out first, slamming the door behind him. The other guy lingered. "Sorry," he said. "He's a good guy, normally. It's just everything that's going on."

"I get it," Clay said. These kinds of assholes wanted empathy for their tough situation. Clay just wanted them out of the car.

The guy pulled out his phone, signing off on the ride. "The weird thing is, he actually is a cop. I don't know why he's dressing like that. Why anybody is. It makes me sick."

***

Clay had earned a break. He got a coffee and a sandwich and treated himself to the luxury of rejecting a handful of ride requests and thinking of nothing much at all.

He'd honed the latter to a skill. Dissociating made days go by easier. Maybe that's why people still wore their Halloween costumes; one more step toward detachment. Clay didn't believe the dress-up cop, though: nothing could keep the hauntings away. It was a conviction that dwelt on the back of his tongue, where the taste of brass burned. Everyone who was haunted (and everybody was) either needed or deserved it. They were all culpable. Smashing apart a wraith wouldn't change that. Disguising yourself wouldn't either.

Clay paused at a ride request that was pinging from a block away: no picture, but the name Joe Palomar was attached to it.

Joe was petite and compact, and Joe had soft brown skin, and Joe had given Clay a handjob that was almost transcendent back in the summer, when Clay was still cruising his passengers. Clay had wondered aloud how anyone could give a handjob that was inspiring rather than perfunctory, and Joe had smiled and said, "The only good thing I learned at Methodist summer camp." Joe had told him to look him up, and Clay never had, because right after that he'd encountered the crying Republican wannabe porn star and realized that being alone was better. Easier, certainly. Detach and dissociate: a survival mechanism for the modern age.

But what, exactly, had detaching gotten him?

Clay accepted the ride, and the Flock app sang its tinny song of praise. "Yeah, yeah," Clay said, and turned the car back on. Joe was only a block away, going to the university's library, and he hadn't seemed the type to try and drag Halloween past its expiration date. Clay was relieved to spot Joe wearing a green hoodie under a brown jacket; no costume in sight, unless it was an extremely subtle one.

"Schiele Library?" Clay asked.

Joe looked up from his phone. "I wondered if it would be you," he said. He sounded pleased rather than annoyed, to Clay's relief. He got in the passenger seat, next to Clay instead of in the backseat. "It's good to see you," he said.

Clay stole glances at Joe as he drove: noted the empty holes that dotted his ear, where Clay remembered delicate silver hoops; noted the stubble on his jaw, the overgrown curls of his hair, and that his skin looked rougher, paler than the ruddy brown of his memory. He looked softer in some places, harder in others.

"How've you been?" Joe asked.

"Can't complain," Clay said. "How are you?"

"The world's fucked," Joe said, though he didn't sound concerned. "Rent's due. Paycheck's late. I've been living off the candy at the receptionist's desk at work. I'm considering selling plasma, but my sister's got me paranoid about the nefarious magical shit that could be done with it. And a cute dude I fooled around with ghosted me."

"…Sorry," Clay said. He actually was.

Joe slouched down and propped his knee up on dashboard. "Don't be. You just said you couldn't complain, and I thought, really? You can't find something to be mad about right now?"

"I think if I let myself get mad," Clay said, "I wouldn't be able to feel anything else."

"My life in a nutshell for the last month or two," Joe said. He blew on his hands to warm them. "I'm holding my shit together with masking tape and spite."

Clay turned up the heat and asked, "You want some of my coffee?"

"Thank you for recognizing that I am actually that desperate," Joe said. After a moment and several sips of coffee, he added, "And sorry if I made it weird."

"It was already a weird day." He pondered telling Joe about the wraiths, the dress-up cop, Natasha, the keys in his throat, then settled on: "My neighbor asked me to talk to her boyfriend about getting pegged."

"Oh my *god*," Joe said. "Do you mean Mari? She asked me the same goddamn thing."

"Are you serious?" Clay wasn't sure if he should be insulted that he wasn't even Mari's first choice. "Wait, how do you know Mari?"

"I started working at the suicide hotline with her," Joe said. "Technically, it's an internship, but it pays, so—what? Why are you laughing?"

***

Clay considered calling it quits after dropping Joe off at Schiele Library, after finding out he'd be at Mari's tonight, after Joe said, "I'm gonna take the rest of your coffee, but I sincerely promise to get you back sometime. Not like that. Unless you're into it."

But Clay had promised that he'd pick up five rides, and he'd already skimped. He was driving back downtown when he saw the group standing in a rough semicircle. They wore costumes: a pirate with a flimsy tricorner hat, a vampire in a tight black dress and torn stockings, a young girl with the green toga and crown of the Statue of Liberty. Clay slowed down as the Statue of Liberty tore a piece of black fabric away and held it above her head, waving it joyfully. The black cloth was being unwound from a wraith, which lay on the ground, curled protectively around itself. Indigo and violet light bled from its eyes, nostrils, and fingertips and pooled on the sidewalk. Droplets caught on the black cloth and splashed onto the hands and clothes of the people surrounding it.

Even from inside the car, Clay could smell sulfur. He could hear, like a ringing in his ears, the wraith's voice as it screamed or cried or sang.

The vampire turned and saw him watching. She had a scrap of the fabric in her hands, and as he watched she wound it around her neck, pulled up one end in an approximation of a noose. *I see you*, she mouthed.

Clay pulled back into traffic, nearly clipping an oncoming car. It was several minutes before the roaring in his ears died down enough for him to hear the chimes from his phone, the Flock app activating and ringing with pleas for rides. He killed the app and at the next red light turned the phone off entirely. His hands were shaking, and shivers ran from the nape of his neck to his gut.

He was okay, he told himself. He hadn't said anything or tried to stop them. They weren't ashamed. They had torn into a wraith in broad daylight, so why did it matter? He had only watched.

Jesus, he had *watched.*

Clay was turning down Owen Avenue when he felt it coming on as a cold sweat, his guts going liquid and then cramping. He pulled over again, jerking the car to a stop and throwing it into park. He fumbled with the door handle and managed to get it open before he doubled over, gagging, choking on the cold metal in his throat. He was sure that he was about to die; he'd be found with stiff limbs and blue skin, or maybe black cloth would wind around his limbs and face, enshroud him. What color light would he bleed?

Clay reached into his mouth, fingertips brushing the very tip of the key, an ecstasy of fumbling before he managed to grasp it. The metal teeth clawed at his throat as he extracted it, but he could breathe again. The cold air burned as he sucked it into his lungs and sobbed.

Clay took one raspy breath and then another, until he could stand to open his eyes and look at the key. It was old, black, and made of iron. There was blood in the creases of his fingers. The taste of metal in his mouth wasn't just from the key; its teeth must have broken the skin.

***

The TV was still on in Mari's apartment. Clay stood on the landing in front of her door, one foot on the stairs going up. He took another step, then turned around and knocked.

"What's wrong?" she asked, when she answered. "Are you okay?"

Clay shook his head. "I'm fine," he tried to say, but his throat rebelled, and the words were a whisper. He thought of Natasha and the tearing sound of her voice. "Water?" he mouthed.

She pulled him into the apartment and filled up a glass of water from the faucet. The first swallow was too large, and the sharp, stabbing pain nearly made him spit it out. Mari's voice seemed to have receded, though he could still hear the TV: a serious voice with a

British accent describing flocks of birds that descended like locusts on farms in sub-Sahara Africa. The birds ate and ate, stripped crops down to barren fields, devouring every seed and plant. It did no good to shoot at them, since they would just rise up, circle around the sky like a dark, buzzing cloud, and land again. Mari turned the TV off. She wrapped a soft blanket around his shoulders and sat him down on the living room couch.

"Can you tell me what happened?" Mari asked.

He focused on her face: the dark-rimmed glasses, the wide, soft nose, the dark freckles that spattered her round cheeks. He opened his mouth to speak, but the pain got in the way. He pulled the metal key from his pocket instead and tapped it on his throat. He wondered if she would forgive him if he told her what he had witnessed, and that he had chosen to drive away from it. He was thankful that he'd lost his voice and wouldn't have to find out.

"I got three postcards yesterday. Four the day before. They're coming more often. I can't—" She closed her mouth. The emotions that were written so clearly on her face fell away, as if she were consciously pulling them off her skin.

"You're not going back outside, are you?" she asked.

He shook his head.

"Good. You should stay for dinner. Come help me cook," Mari said, then suddenly sat up straight. "Fuck, I hope I didn't burn the onions."

She had, in fact, burnt the crap out of the onions, and the kitchen was filled with greasy, acrid smoke. Mari swore while wiping tears out of her eyes, and Clay coughed and winced.

"Fuck *everything*," Mari shouted. She opened the back door and threw the pan, heedless of the oil that splattered on her arms. It flew end over end, and a few blackened onions came loose and arced out in their own orbits before hitting the ground.

They opened every window and tried to wave the smoke outside, but the smell lingered. "Fuck," Mari said again. "This doesn't mean everything is ruined, right? It's not a sign."

Clay shook his head, not sure if he believed himself. He could believe it for Mari's sake, he thought. "It's just a pan," he tried to say, but he couldn't speak around the smoke in his throat. He typed the words out on his phone instead: *Just a pan.*

Mari sighed, then coughed and wiped her face. "It feels like everything is life or death these days. Even a shitty pan from IKEA."

Let's just make food, he wrote. Then, because he knew it would make her smile, added some stupid emojis: ramen noodles, muscle arm, praise hands. Mari rolled her eyes, but she got out another pan. First onions, then ginger and garlic. Mung beans and shrimp stock, water, then the shrimp themselves, already cooked to a tender, pale pink. Mari put the fish in the oven—she'd planned to fry it, but said darkly that she no longer trusted the stove. Clay took care of the rice. The kitchen still smelled acrid, but it also now smelled like the sea, like something distant and comfortingly vast.

Finn arrived first, bearing a six-pack of fancy beer and a salad whose lettuce was buried under small hills of nuts, seeds, dried fruits, and avocado slices. He opened a beer and offered another to Clay, who shook his head, gestured to his throat. One good thing: he wouldn't have to talk to Finn about taking it up the butt for a day or two.

The apartment began to fill with people, not uncomfortably so, just bodies occupying places that had seemed empty before. The house warmed up, and the smell of burnt onions was overlaid with the smell of people, beer, wine, cheese, bread, casseroles.

Joe arrived last, bearing cookies still steaming with heat and the scent of almonds and cardamom. "Sorry I'm so late. It took longer than I thought to bake them," he said.

Clay smiled and managed a whispered "Hey."

"Are you okay?" Joe said. "Did something happen?"

Long story, he mouthed.

"I can't promise this'll make it better, but…" Joe handed him one of the cookies. Clay broke off a piece and held it in his mouth, surprised at its softness—sweet and buttery with the tang of ginger. Clay imagined that taste on Joe's tongue, should he kiss him, and felt something like lust, something like affection.

They all ate in the living room, since Mari only had a shaky card table with a janky leg. The only thing Clay could eat was Mari's soup, which stung his throat in a soothing way, salty as tears. He sat on the couch, and Joe sat on the ground next to him, his shoulder resting gently against one of Clay's legs, warm and solid.

Inevitably, Mari's coworkers started talking about the suicide hotline. They'd fielded more than two hundred calls in the last week, and nearly as many text messages. Mari had talked to a couple of teens and repeated the stories they told her: that kids at their schools still wore Halloween costumes, even though they were stained and smelled like sweat; some of the teachers had started to dress up too, or wear plastic masks. Wraiths were filling up the bleachers and the back rows of classrooms.

After a while, there was nothing more to say about it. The conversation broke up, fracturing into smaller discussions around the room.

Joe was a warm weight on his leg. What was he haunted by, Clay wondered? Joe turned to look at him and gave him a soft smile, then whispered, "I think one of Mari's dildos is going to get its wings tonight."

Clay snorted a laugh, and then winced. Mari and Finn were engaged in a close, whispered conversation, spoken mostly into each other's ears. Finn was flushed, and Mari looked smug. Maybe Finn had gotten over his ass-related anxieties on his own.

Guests started drifting out. Mari put Finn and Joe on dish duty while Clay gathered up empty beer bottles and took out the garbage. Night had fallen, crisp and clear, and a fat, generous moon hung in the sky. As Clay climbed back up the stairs to Mari's balcony, something caught his eye: lights moving through the fields beyond their backyard.

He'd never noticed that the lights that dripped and seeped from the wraiths were different colors, as unique as bruises: indigo, pale violet, hints of green or blue. Dozens of wraiths were gathering around the old construction site, alighting on the frozen machines. The lights fell like water as the wraiths moved across the field.

"Clay. Get back in the house."

Clay turned. Joe was standing on the balcony, one hand urgently beckoning him, the other holding his phone to his ear.

"I am telling him," Joe said, and Clay realized that he was talking into the phone. "Clay, come inside now."

Clay looked again: beyond the field of swaying, sloshing lights, groups of costumed people were walking down the road that led to town. He could hear the murmur of their voices, the jagged edges of laughter. Was the cop down there? What about the monkey girl from last night, or the group of kids that had tortured the wraith? Joe grabbed Clay by the hand and pulled him back inside, locking the door behind them. Mari had turned off all the lights.

"Should we shut the blinds?" Finn asked.

Mari said, "What if they see the movement?"

They sat on the floor, pulling blankets and pillows off the couch to make it comfortable. Joe was still talking urgently into the phone. "It's okay," he said. "We're safe. Safe enough for now. I know, it's all right. You'll find it someday. It's—you what?"

He looked at Clay, then back at the ground. "Why?" he asked. "I don't think that's a good idea. Look, just tell me—damn it."

He put his phone in his pocket and told the rest of them, "Third time she's called today. Has it been happening to the rest of you more often?"

Joe was haunted by phone calls. It seemed so pedestrian, not to mention easy to ignore. But you ignored the hauntings at your peril. As Joe leaned against the couch, he pulled his phone back out, staring at it, waiting for it to ring. At least Clay's keys didn't demand answers from him. He tried to imagine the other side of Joe's conversation: Are you safe? How safe? For how long? How can you be sure?

***

He wasn't sure when he fell asleep, or when exactly he woke up, coaxed back into consciousness with Joe's body pressed against him, Joe's mouth. Such a change from waking up with the sharp pressure of metal teeth against the back of his tongue. It felt good to be disoriented this way, to not know who had started kissing whom. Maybe that's what he could tell Finn about bottoming: it would push buttons you didn't know you had, sure, but it could also be such an easy, sweet release.

Although now that he was listening for it, he could hear noises from the direction of Mari's bedroom, raised in unselfconscious pleasure. He wasn't going to speculate on what they were doing in there, but he hoped they felt as good as he did.

There was a pinging sound. "Sorry," Joe said, as he broke away and fumbled for his phone. But the noise was coming from Clay's phone, and he recognized the sound of the alert: a Flock passenger asking for a ride.

"That's me," he said. The pain in his throat had settled to a burning ache, but flared when he spoke. Clay pulled the app up on his phone, ready to reject it and sign off, when he saw the name and the picture: a woman with long dark hair, smiling in soft, warm light, sunglasses covering her face. Natasha.

"I should take this," he whispered, though the words felt like splinters in his throat.

"What is that?" Joe said. Clay showed him the phone, and the look of half-asleep desire dropped from Joe's face. "Tasha?"

He took Clay's phone from him, and the light illuminated his face, the planes and curves of it. Clay wondered how he hadn't seen it before, the resemblance between the two of them. She wasn't a wraith; she was Joe's haunting.

"She wanted to talk to you tonight," Joe said.

Clay nodded. "Do you want to come?"

Joe shook his head. "It's so hard, just hearing her voice. I don't know if I can."

"It's all right," Clay said, though he wasn't convinced that was true.

"Tell her I'm sorry," Joe said, giving Clay back the phone. "Tell her I'm sorry I couldn't do more."

Clay pulled on his jacket, scarf, and boots. He contemplated kissing Joe again before he left, but Joe had turned toward the wall, phone clenched in his hand.

The field and abandoned construction site were empty. Down by the holes where the foundations would never be poured, a single, solitary figure was waiting. Clay stood silently, watching her, until the phone in his hand pinged again. He still hadn't accepted the ride request.

He did so, and as he was shoving his phone into his pocket, the balcony door opened. Joe came out, coat open, boots untied. He grabbed Clay's hand and held it until they got to the car.

***

Ride number five.

Clay drove out to where he'd picked up Natasha that morning and honked once, apologetically, but she didn't move. There were no fences, so Clay turned and drove directly onto the field itself, hoping the muddy ground had frozen over.

Natasha no longer wore the sunglasses, scarf, or hat, but Clay found himself unable to look directly at her face; his gaze fell, instead, to the rusty stains along the hem and sleeves of her coat, the frayed knot of her dark hair.

Finally, abandoning her contemplation of the pit, the moon, or whatever she'd been looking at, Natasha came over to the car. Her limp was not as pronounced, and she didn't move with the same slowness and caution as she had before. She reached for the passenger-side door, but stopped when she saw Joe. She left a handprint on the window, a smear that could have been dirt or blood, and got into the backseat.

They waited for her to speak, and eventually she did.

"When it happened," she said. "When they took my skin, they left my eyes. I can't look away. I see all of it. I see what I am, and what I used to be, and how everything has changed."

"I'm sorry," Joe said. She scoffed. The sound was wet, choked, bloody. Clay flinched and saw that Joe didn't; he must have been used to this.

Her voice dragged down to a hoarse whisper. "Do you have the key?"

Blood was pooling at the bottom of her eyelids, gathering on her lashes. The car was filling with the smell of rust, metal, salt, blood. The key he'd nearly choked on that afternoon was still in his pocket. Clay patted it to be sure.

"We'll need it," Natasha said.

"Where are we going?" Joe asked.

"Nowhere just yet," she said. "We need to wait for them."

"Who?"

She pointed out the window. After a moment, the lights of the dead surged upward, more numerous than Clay had ever seen or imagined, rising up out of the ground like clumsy, hungry birds.

BEFORE WE DISPERSE LIKE STAR STUFF

Part One: Damian

Are we rolling? Should I…yeah, okay. My name is Damian Flores. I'm an activist with a degree in environmental archeology, which is basically the study of how prehistoric humans interacted with and related to their environments. I left academia because, well. If you study how humans have dealt with changing climates in the past, you start getting a little concerned about the future, right? Or like, a lot concerned. I lose a lot of sleep thinking about the next hundred years.

This activism is what…well, I guess we'll talk about that more in depth later, right? So should I just…launch into the spiel?

Okay, here is what we know. Sometime in the late Pliocene era—

Sorry, what? Sure, that makes sense. From the top?

Here is what we know. Or theorize, I should probably say theorize. You think? Ray and Min would say…

Okay, here is what we know. Around three and a half million years ago, there was a species of weasels, Megalictis ossicarminis, that looked like a cross between river otters and wolverines. They had human-level intelligence and a complex social organization. They lived together, they caught and shared food, they used tools, they even collected shiny rocks.

In simpler terms: they were people. Before humans were people. People before being a person was cool.

And they left behind messages.

Was that okay? I can probably make it sound more...Yeah, let's shoot it again.

***

The elevator doors closed behind him, and in their mirrored shine, Damian saw two things: a hot guy, well-dressed in a suit tailored to his short frame, and a fucking sellout.

He grinned, trying the expression out, then clamped his mouth shut in a grimace. He'd gotten his teeth whitened for this meeting, and they looked too bright. It was strangely close to the dysphoria he'd had before he transitioned, a sense of searching his reflection for something that didn't feel weird and off-putting. And sure, his shoes were made of recycled materials, from a company that did one-to-one donations; the underwear he wore was fair-trade organic cotton; and his tie was made by an upstart genderqueer fashionista making a living off their Etsy. Under his shirt, the ugly-ass pendant that his mother had made hung between his mirrored mastectomy scars, and below that a tattooed line of poetry his grandfather had written as a teenager in Havana.

But all of the insignia of Damian's complicated self were beneath the surface. He *looked* like a sellout.

"Get it together," he told his reflection. His reflection nodded back. *We're on the same side, bro*, it seemed to say. Damian wasn't convinced.

The door opened on the twenty-second floor, and Damian hung a right, past the wall of windows looking out on Lower Manhattan, and then onward to his agent's office. Amelia was waiting for him in her Power Suit regalia, corporate-femme mode fully activated.

"Nice," she said, giving him the once-over. "You clean up well."

"Likewise," he said. "I feel like a..." He trailed off because he wasn't sure he could actually articulate how he felt to Amelia, who wore her outfit like glorious armor. His felt like a heavy costume, constricting and burdensome.

"Don't worry about how you feel in it," she said. "Worry about the impression you make. That's all these meetings are: impressions."

They had four meetings, more or less back-to-back, with different production companies who all wanted to option the book. Amelia did most of the talking. Damian's role was to keep quiet, nod thoughtfully, and maybe ask a few pointed questions.

The first three studios basically pitched him different versions of the same story—*his* story: an intrepid activist/scientist discovers a cave full of the fossilized remains of an ancient non-human society. ("We're in talks with the team that did *Avatar*. The effects are gonna be…just, wow.") The cave is in danger of being destroyed by an Evil Corporation. ("Tommy Lee Jones has expressed an interest in playing the villainous CEO.") The intrepid activist/scientist and his team come up with a daring plan to save the cave and the land around it, nearly fail when they realize the Evil Corporation is even more evil than previously assumed, but at the last possible second, pull it off. Huzzah!

The teams from the studios threw in various subplots. All of them featured a straight love interest. (One of them had read enough to mention Min by name, though casually mentioned that they'd be trying to find an actress "as close to Emma Stone as possible.") There was also a mother-with-cancer subplot, a gay coming-out subplot—which intrigued Damian until he realized that they wanted to play it for laughs—and his personal favorite: the non-human society was still alive, living in sewers beneath major American cities, conspiring to take back the planet.

After Amelia gently shooed out the last set, the two of them regarded each other across the conference table.

"I work with activists who start meetings with guided meditations so everyone can open their heart chakras," Damian said. "And that's still less bullshit than what we just sat through."

"Damian," Amelia said.

"I feel *dirty*." He flapped his hands, as if he could peel the feeling from his skin and flick it off. "Did any of them even read the book?"

"Of course they didn't," Amelia snapped. "They read a plot synopsis that their assistants typed up for them. They're not book people, they're movie people."

"I'm pretty sure they were goddamn *lizard* people," Damian said. There was a knock at the door. He looked at Amelia—was there another meeting? But she looked as surprised as he did. The door opened and...

Damian's first impression was the guy from *Ancient Aliens*, the one who had been turned into a meme. Tall with unruly hair, an ill-fitting tweed suit, and a pair of narrow, steel-rimmed glasses perched on the end of a nose as severe as a Roman senator's. The second impression was, okay, maybe that guy's sister? Cousin? Co-author?

The woman settled herself into one of the chairs, pulled out half a dozen manila folders and three separate notebooks, and started talking in the sort of uninterrupted flow that spoke to either a healthy cocaine habit or an unhealthy amount of enthusiasm.

"I've got to say, it's an honor to meet you, Mister Flores. I've been dreaming about this meeting. Literally dreaming about it. Usually it's an anxiety dream and I'm naked or my teeth are falling out." She actually looked down at herself, apparently for reassurance.

"Hi?" Damian said. He looked to Amelia for help, and she stepped in.

"I'm sorry, I seem to have..." She pawed through her notes. "Would you mind telling me your name again?"

"Annika Wagner-Smith. From the Smithsonian network?"

That got Damian's attention. "The Smithsonian?"

Annika nodded, and her swoop of ashy hair bobbed as she did so. "I know that we left things open after our email exchange, Ms. Fontaine, but I've been working on the proposal, and I don't mind telling you that there's been a *lot* of executive interest about this documentary."

"A documentary," Damian said. "Not a movie?"

"*Movies*," Annika scoffed. "We're not interested in regurgitating tired old narratives. The discovery of *Megalictis ossicarminis* forced us to radically reconsider sapience, evolution, and civilization. Our network wants to delve into not just the nitty-gritty of their discovery, but what this *means* for us, as humans."

She slapped a glossy printout onto the table and slid it over to them.

"Holy shit," Damian said. He'd seen artists' renderings of *ossicarminis* before. Hell, he'd looked over a dozen when the publisher was putting together his book. But there was something about these images that gave them, for lack of a better term, *life*. They didn't look like chubby weasels with a shiny rock and a bone. They looked… well, they looked badass. And maybe it was bad science, but it was really cool to see a prehistoric weasel the size of mountain lion dressed like a minor character in He-Man.

"Why does it say *Space Weasels* across the top?" Amelia said.

"It's a working title," Annika shrugged.

Damian and Amelia looked at each other. "*Ossicarminis* wasn't—"

"It's a theory that one of the executive producers is interested in investigating," Annika said smoothly. She slid another printout toward them. This one had *ossicarminis* at the helm of, god help them all, what looked like the bridge of the USS *Enterprise*. Several other *ossicarminis* were pointing excitedly toward a planet. "It's not going to be the focus of the documentary, but our audiences are going to wonder why we'd be leaving out this particular theory."

"Theory that...*ossicarminis* went to space?" Damian asked.

Annika shrugged again. "Our audiences like space."

***

"You can't be serious," Amelia said, once they were safely en-sconced at a tapas place an hour later. Damian had decided to wait until their second round of drinks before telling Amelia that he want-ed Annika to have the movie rights.

"Everyone else wanted to turn this into a shitty Spielberg block-buster. It's not that kind of story."

"How is *Indiana Jones and the Underground Weasel Society* worse that *Weasels from Space?*"

"Indiana Jones is Orientalist garbage. Weasels from space is at least *different.*"

Amelia pursed her lips. "Different is a very, *very* kind interpreta-tion. Would Ray and Min agree to it?"

Damian took a long, measured sip of his margarita. He had managed to avoid thinking about Ray Walker and Min-ji Hong—the two people who technically co-discovered *ossicarminis* with him—for the entire meeting, and honestly, for most of the last year and a half, while he'd been touring the book and lecturing (incidentally, not anywhere that came within fifty miles of either of them).

Amelia leaned forward. "If you do go the documentary route, you'll need both of them on board. And it's going to be up to you to convince them, not the Smithsonian."

He didn't ask why they needed to be there: the three of them had co-authored the definitive paper about *ossicarminis* before...well, before he'd signed a contract to write *The Oracle Bones: What an Inhu-man Society Can Tell Us about Being Human* by himself. "Why is that up to me?" he asked.

"Because they deserve to hear it from you, not some fluffy-haired wingnut with fursona art of space weasels."

"I liked the art!" Damian said. Amelia stared him down, and he shrank into the booth. "Okay, I get your point."

***

I got called to the site by a Midwest anti-fracking coalition. The thing is, protected land that's owned by the government isn't really protected; the government can basically sell it off to the highest bidder, unless they've got a really pressing reason not to. The Nebraska Energy and Oil Commission were getting ready to hand over a few thousand acres in the Pine Ridge area, and a local community coalition called me in to see if there were fossils—something they could use to get the public riled up about protecting the land from development.

There were fossils, mostly from the Pliocene, but it was all fish and ferns. People only really get excited about human remains and dinosaurs. Blame Jurassic Park and our innate self-centeredness.

It's pure accident that I found the cave. I literally fell into it. It had been covered at some point by siltstone, probably from millenia of floods, and something had weakened the ground enough that I just fell through.

I wasn't immediately sure what I was seeing. The skeletons were half-buried in more siltstone, bones sticking out at odd angles. I could see they were big, but not human. But then I caught sight of the oracles. There's no way to mistake that for anything but writing. Symbols carved into bones, darkened with walnut dye. They looked older than anything I'd ever seen. I called Min in right away, the same day, I think, once I got out of the cave. I thought I'd hit the jackpot, because that was evidence of human activity, right? And it was!

We can't know for certain, but yeah, I think that the ossicarminis skeletons were buried with purpose, rather than died in that position.

The arrangement of the two bodies, the placement of the stones and the oracles, none of that was accidental.

Ah. Ah, yeah. Yeah, that—I guess you could call that a controversy. But like—

Ray said that, huh? I think "disturbing the dead" is, uh, some very... particular language. Oh fuck, did I really say that? Gross. Don't print that. Let me try again.

***

Everyone had assured Damian that selling movie rights practically guaranteed that nothing would happen soon, but that was not the way Annika Wagner-Smith worked. She wanted to start shooting immediately.

Damian decided to go see Min in Chicago, but only after five emails, seven texts, and three calls went unanswered. The Smithsonian agreed to pick up the bill, with Annika and her crew out there to do some preliminary shooting. The actual oracle bones were kept at the University of Chicago, and if Min agreed, they'd want some shots of her examining them, plus pickups of the campus and the city. Annika also said she had an idea for an opening sequence.

Three more texts and one phone call later, Damian dropped in on her advisor to see if Min was still alive. "She's revising her dissertation, so, for a given value of *alive*..." said Professor Rinaldi. (*Fucking academics,* Damian thought.) Rinaldi gave Damian her address and advised him to bring her coffee and food. Damian picked up some iced coffee and noodles at the Korean place down the street from Min's, then knocked gingerly at her door.

He had trouble reconciling the creature that emerged from the darkened apartment as the Min he'd known as an adult: hair greasy, glasses askew (hadn't she switched to contacts?), rumpled, smelly. She'd spent years honing her femininity the same way that Damian had his masculinity—partly out of desire, partly out of defense, so gender wasn't the first or only thing someone saw about you. Now, Min looked like she'd regressed back to those late-summer days at Camp Transcendent, when the two of them were baby trans having acoustic singalongs to old queercore songs and trying to figure out what gender, like, even *was*.

"Damian?" she said blearily. "Are you here or am I hallucinating from sleep deprivation?"

He smiled magnanimously at her. "Not only am I here, I brought you sustenance."

She opened the door and held out her hands. Damian deposited the coffee and takeout container into them, then followed her into the apartment, which smelled like musty armpits, dirty dishes, and fake strawberries.

"Don't sit on anything that looks integral to my research," Min said. Papers and books littered nearly every surface. Damian decided to stand.

"I was worried you were dead. I sent a bunch of texts and never heard back," he said.

Min shrugged as she set the food down. "I had to finish revising. I put everything that might distract me in my old trunk, locked it, and gave my mom the key."

"Even your phone?"

"Even my sex toys."

Damian refused to imagine Mrs. Hong getting too curious about the contents of her daughter's locked trunk. "Well, I'm glad you're not dead."

"That makes one of us," Min muttered. She slurped at the coffee, then pulled out an e-cig and puffed a plume of sweet vapor. That explained the weird strawberry smell.

"Is this about the documentary thing?" she asked.

Damian nodded. "Did Amelia call you before you locked your phone up?"

Min shook her head. "My mom told me. She's been reading my texts and voicemails and stuff, and forwarding anything that seems important. She's still mad that you cut me out of the book deal, but she thought she'd let me make up my own mind about this."

It was on the tip of his tongue to ask if Min herself was still mad, but he was too afraid that she would say yes. Anyway, this wasn't about him. This was about *ossicarminis*, one of the biggest and most underreported discoveries in evolution. It was about the land where they'd been found, which was still under threat of development. It was only very marginally about Damian proving to himself that he wasn't a complete sellout.

"Anyway," he said. "Documentary? Are you interested?"

"If they pay me, sure. I helped discover a nonhuman writing system, but I still haven't found a fucking postdoc fellowship." She made a pathetic noise and opened the takeout container. "I should have dropped out after *ossicarminis*. Done what you did and speed-written some sensationalist crap by myself, then gone on the talk-show circuit. I'm mostly mad you did it first."

She didn't even sound angry; she'd apparently moved all the way through exhaustion into an affect as flat as the Midwestern horizon.

"Ray would have given you his disappointed face," Damian said. He was very well acquainted with it.

"You survived just fine."

Damian shrugged. "I'm an asshole, though. And your mother would have killed you."

Min shoveled more noodles into her mouth. "At least that would have been quick."

Damian looked around the apartment, noticing that, even amidst the general atmosphere of neglect and disaster, the oracle bones that *ossicarminis* had been named for held pride of place on the mantle.

"Those are nice-looking replicas," he said, moving closer. Ray believed they were from a species of *Teratornis*, giant predatory birds that probably terrorized *ossicarminis*. Damian could still picture that moment: Ray with the carved bones in his gloved hands, twisting them around to run his fingers over the carved sigils, describing an airborne nightmare with fifteen-foot wingspans. The two of them had shared a joint in the bed of Ray's truck later, imagining *ossicarminis* somehow taking down what was probably one of their biggest predators, and using its bones to write incomprehensible messages for an unimaginable future. Then Damian had given him a blowjob. It was a great night. They'd had a lot of great nights before Damian had ruined everything.

Min paused in her slurping. "Replicas," she said. "Yep. That's what those are."

Damian pivoted to look at her. "You *didn't*."

Min shoveled some noodles into her mouth, presumably so she couldn't incriminate herself further.

"Does the university know you have these? Jesus, does *Ray* know you have these?" Damian demanded. For fuck's sake, they weren't even in boxes. The bones were out on her mantle where anyone could see them, take them, *sneeze* on them. This room didn't even have proper humidity control.

Min took her time chewing. "The University has the replicas. I wasn't going to give them the real things and let a bunch of grubby undergrads touch them. Ray…" She let the pause hang for an extended moment, then scooped more noodles into her mouth.

"You know what Ray thinks about this," Damian said. "He wants the skeletons and artifacts re-interred and left alone. He *dumped* me over this, and you—"

"He dumped you for plenty of reasons, and those…" Min pointed with her chopsticks at her mantle. "…aren't one of them, since he doesn't know. You don't get to blame that shit on me, motherfucker."

There was the Min he knew and loved. Damian immediately wanted to ask her what Ray had told her about their breakup. But that was too pathetic, even for him, even in this strange time where Min seemed to have reverted into her smelly, gluttonous teenage self. Instead, he crossed his arms and told her, "You have to give them back."

Min set the noodles on her table amid the piles of papers. "Say what?"

"Not to the university, fuck them." He waved his hand. "But you can't keep them for yourself. That's probably the only thing *worse* than having them stuck in a drawer in the school's archives."

Min groaned and rubbed at her face. "I'll think about it. I'm not promising jack shit right now. I'm a fucking train wreck and I haven't slept in two and a half days." She picked up her noodles again, stabbing her chopsticks into them.

"Fine," Damian said. "But so help me, you are at least going to store the *priceless artifacts* in a goddamn protective microclimate." He looked at the window and felt a righteous fury surge through him. "For fuck's sake, do you leave these in direct sunlight?"

***

Min managed to transform herself back into mostly human shape for the possible opening sequence the next day. For some ungodly reason, they were shooting in the Loop during the midday lunch rush. Nothing said humanity like swarms of office workers descending on a Corner Bakery, apparently. Damian had to hurry to keep pace with Min; she was six inches taller than him and, when thrust onto a busy sidewalk, walked like she'd been sent to kill someone but wouldn't mind racking up a body count along the way.

"They're going to do some shoots in San Francisco next, at the *ossicarminis* exhibit," Damian said, because he and Min were supposed to be making friendly conversation in the shot. Min nodded, barely listening, more enthralled with her Venti Frappuccino. Did everyone finish their PhD with a lethal caffeine habit, or just the assholes Damian loved and had surrounded himself with? "We get a retainer and all expenses paid. Apparently they want to interview all three of us about the exhibit."

"So Ray's on board." Technically a statement, but there was a healthy amount of skepticism in her voice.

"I'm working on it," Damian said. "I'll be flying down to Kansas tonight."

Annika, who was walking backward while looking at the screen, leaving her harried assistant director to make sure she didn't step on a tourist or a pile of dogshit, called out, "I need the two of you to liven it up a little! You look like you're on your way to a funeral."

"Mine, probably," Damian said drily.

That made Min laugh.

"Good, yes, more like that!" Annika called.

After fifteen minutes of the two of them walking and trying not to look at the camera, they and the crew moved to the Field Museum.

"I don't think I've been here since my second-worst Tinder date," said Min. "What was that, five years ago?"

"Six," Damian said, remembering it well. Min had detailed the whole thing in a long Tumblr post that later went viral.

"Okay, okay, our stand-in performer should be meeting us here," Annika said, coming up to them. She handed them their tickets and then checked her smart watch.

"Stand-in?" Damian asked.

"We'll be bringing *ossicarminis* to life in this scene. The little rascal will be following you through the museum. Plus we'll have some web-exclusive extras that will look like *Night at the Museum*, except—ah! Herman!"

Annika waved to a chubby white kid, probably sixteen at most, with pink cheeks and an ill-advised man bun. He was short, a couple inches shorter than Damian. And underneath a light jacket and a pair of basketball shorts, he was wearing bright green spandex leggings.

"Who's that?" Min whispered to Damian.

"That's my nephew," Annika replied. She apparently had the ears of a school librarian. "He'll be playing the stand-in for the CGI *ossicarminis*."

She hugged and kissed the boy on the cheek, and he put up with it as graciously as a teenager could. Annika clapped her hands.

"Okay, so, we're going to start in here. I'd like Min and Damian by the big dinosaur thing," Annika called, gesturing toward Sue the T-Rex. "Herman, you're playing a very mischievous giant weasel. Very smart, a little shy."

"Giant weasel, got it." He yanked off his jacket and basketball shorts and got on all fours. The bright green spandex turned out to be a full onesie.

"Damian," Min said, clutching his arm.

"Yeah."

"This is weird, right? This isn't just me forgetting how to deal with other humans after subsisting on beef jerky and instant coffee for two weeks."

"No, this is genuinely weird." He turned to her. "But it's going to look great on your CV."

He and Min spent the next hour pretending to stalk and be stalked by a teenager in a neon spandex suit while cameras rolled, schoolchildren stared at them, and tourists gave them the stink eye for ruining their photos of the taxidermied man-eating lions of Tsavo. Min was stiff the whole time, wary, and obviously re-acclimating to using her body for anything besides endlessly revising a manuscript. Min had always been in the "when can I download my brain into a robot" camp of trans people.

Damian had dropped academia like a hot, rotten potato after getting his MA and never looked back. He was too goal-oriented for the long con of academic life. He'd fallen gratefully into environmental organizing, finding it infinitely preferable to be in front of a crowd than a classroom. Min, on the other hand, was made for academia. She relentlessly dug for deeper answers, then deeper questions that complicated those answers. It had made her incredibly frustrating to work with, when the two of them and Ray co-wrote their paper on *ossicarminis*. On the other hand, it also meant that her dissertation was probably going to be miles better than Damian's book.

"Okay, okay, okay," Annika chanted as she paced the length of the room. She had a way of doing that, as if she were appeasing a silent, ghostly audience. Or perhaps, more likely, an audience of executives from the Smithsonian. She stood in front of a taxidermied crocodile. "Okay, I need a minute. I've gotten lost and need to figure my way out."

Her assistant frowned and said in a stage whisper, "Let's all take five. Bathroom break. Herman, don't go too far."

The crew wandered off. Min looked around at the empty room, then snuck a hit off her vape.

"Seriously?" Damian hissed. "When did you start vaping anyway?"

"When I had a mental breakdown over switching my dissertation project with no support from my advisor or department, because they're all either jealous or think it's a hoax." Min shrugged. "It's got CBD oil in it. Helps with anxiety."

"Are you anxious right now?" he asked. It was definitely weird to get stalked by a teenager in spandex, but not even the weirdest thing they'd ever done together.

"It's the first time I've been out of my apartment in nearly a month, and I've apparently signed up to be part of a documentary with CGI weasels." She snuck another look around the room, but it was just the two of them and Annika eye-fucking the taxidermied alligator. She pulled another hit off her vape. "But I'm also done with my fucking diss, so I guess I could be worse."

Damian looked at her, his concern growing. "Congratulations. I don't know if I said that already."

"You didn't." She exhaled vapor out her nose. The room filled with silence, occupying the space where it seemed like Min should have said something else, or he should have.

"Could the two of you have your feelings somewhere else?" Annika called. "It's distracting."

There was a set of windows near the Hall of Gems that overlooked Lake Michigan, which glinted with hard flecks of sunlight. Damian peered out while Min leaned against the banister. The camera crew followed them but kept their distance, filming Herman cavorting in his lime-green suit.

Damian wondered how much of Min's dissertation was devoted to discrediting everything he had written in *Oracle Bones*, then wondered if that was self-centered. Min would almost certainly say so. Ray probably wouldn't even deign to answer, just raise a single eyebrow. Ray had a way of making you feel a couple inches tall without even trying very hard.

"Can I read it?" Damian asked instead. "Your dissertation, I mean. I'm sure it's amazing."

Min side-eyed him; her side-eye was vicious, sharp as a scalpel. It was startlingly different to how she'd acted on camera. It was profoundly sad to be playing at having the same friendship that had once sustained them.

"We'll see," she said.

Annika came out of the alligator room, face stretched into a disconcerting smile. She approached both of them and laid a steely grip on each of their shoulders. "I've got it," she said. "I understand how it all works now. It's going to be fantastic." She shook them both a little, like a dog roughing a chew toy. "*We're* going to be fantastic."

Min blinked. "Cool?" she said.

"Off to San Francisco next," she said, releasing them with a decisive move. "We're going to need Doctor Walker there. Damian, do you still want to talk to him yourself? That will need to happen sooner rather than later."

Damian forced a grin onto his face. "Sounds great. Fantastic. Can't wait."

***

I'm sorry, what? Who would win in a fight? Smilodon and ossicarminis didn't even exist at the same time. They wouldn't have fought. Even if they did exist at the same time, which is not in the fossil record…I don't care if you've already started plotting this sequence, I'm not going to sign off on ossicarminis fighting a saber-toothed tiger. I'm definitely not going to have an opinion about it. This is a serious documentary about a serious topic, and—

Ray said what? Of course he did. God. He may be a scientist, but he's also such a dude sometimes.

***

Damian's book tour had taken him all over the US. Before that, he'd been into the lecture circuit, convincing liberal arts colleges to give him money in exchange for making science and environmental activism look like a sexy, valid career choice. It wasn't the first time he'd come through Kansas, but it was definitely the first time he'd come this far into it, flying into Kansas City and driving two hours west. He stopped for a quick burger and pee break at a place called Spangles, and had to squeeze past a statue of Elvis on his way to the bathroom. He felt nervous in the stall; nobody had given him shit about using the men's room in three or four years, but a place where they hung guitars on the walls emblazoned with *God Bless America* seemed likely to break the streak.

Emporia, once he got there, was a little better. It was a Midwest college town—significantly scaled down, but it had the same array of cutesy shops, grotty bars, and the odd bookstore and tattoo parlor that he'd come to expect. It wasn't bedazzled, airbrushed AMERICA. Thank fuck.

Damian killed half an hour at a local coffee shop, hoping the heat and familiarity of a hazelnut latte would calm his nerves. Instead, he ceaselessly imagined all of the things that he'd say to Ray, immediately forgot them in his panic, and then panicked even more because he couldn't face Ray without an idea of what to say. He should have called. He should have let Annika or one of the producers handle this. He shouldn't have sold out! Or maybe he should never have kissed Ray on a clear, moonlit night, when they were both buzzed from a spliff and a court order halting the development.

By the time he found Ray's office, Damian was in a state of acute misery, sweating because Kansas apparently hadn't gotten the memo that it was April and not August. The door was locked. A post-it note said Dr. Walker was out in the field.

The department secretary informed him that Ray was doing a population study with his students in the Flint Hills. She pursed her lips as she told him this, as if Damian were a recalcitrant student who hadn't done his homework, and wow, that brought back memories. Luckily, Damian had learned to ooze the sort of charm that was weirdly effective on academic staff and professors. The secretary eventually gave him written directions to the place in Flint Hills where Ray was apparently counting antelope.

It always weirded Damian out that you could drive seventy-five or eighty miles an hour through most of Kansas legally. Humans weren't meant to go past sixty-five, in his opinion, and he had to consciously relax his white-knuckle grip as he forced the speedometer up to seventy. Even then, massive Ford pickup trucks were whizzing past him in the left lane. He gritted his teeth and forced himself not to swerve. Hitting a tree on the straightest road on the damn continent would be an embarrassing way to die.

The Kansas landscape stretched flat in all directions, disrupted by hay bales and the odd muddy creek or copse of trees. It was a little prettier once he got closer to the park, but Damian had yet to spot any hills, flint or otherwise. He found the turnoff after several minutes of searching, doubling back, and prayer, and followed the long dirt track to a lean-to in the middle of a field. A half-dozen cars were parked in the flattened grass, several sporting Emporia State stickers. Still, Damian wasn't certain he'd found what he was looking for until he saw Ray's truck. The sight of the boxy blue Toyota hit him like a fist to the solar plexus, as if his nostalgia had mass and velocity, shooting out in a soft arc before coming around like a boomerang and knocking him on his ass. How many nights had he passed in that truck? How many days had he spent riding in its cab, sandwiched between his best friend and the man he was dizzily, annoyingly in love with?

***

Ray was still out in the field, so Damian practiced his charm on Ray's unsuspecting undergrads. About half of them actually recognized him, and the rest were happy to be distracted from data entry with the story of how he had met Ray. He'd been practicing it, figuring he would be telling it on camera in the near future.

"I got my names mixed up. There's a paleontologist in Omaha with the same name but different spelling, and I thought I was calling him at first. Ray was less than a year into his tenure, and the department secretary literally asked me if I wouldn't rather talk to one of the senior professors."

"Doctor Pratt is still really salty about that," one of the students said, grinning.

"Yeah, you can't ask him to be on the same committee as Ray anymore. He gets really bitchy about it," another added.

Damian grinned. "Not surprised. He called me on the dig and actually told me that if I was smart, I'd ask him to take over." He'd actually been in Ray's truck, and put Pratt on speaker phone so that Ray could listen to him talk his entitled shit in person. Right up until he dropped some barely veiled racist bullshit about Ray's standoffishness and unreliability, then launched into a rant about how the department was being diminished by "minority hires" like Ray, who was Lakota. Damian hung up on Pratt and used the fucker's university email to sign up for newsletters from several pornography and fetish sites.

"Anyway," he said, "I had to email Doctor Walker six more times and then pester the department secretary before he'd agree to a Skype meeting. I'm pretty sure he only agreed so he could tell me to my face to fuck off," Damian finished, to a generous round of laughter. Of course, that's when Ray walked up. Damian couldn't have planned it better.

"What the hell are you doing here?" Ray said, which killed the laughter as sharply as if it had been guillotined.

Ray spoke in a flat Midwest accent that, for some reason, always made Damian think of hollow logs rolling down a hill. It was unmistakable and weirdly attractive.

"I was hoping to talk to you," Damian answered. He put his hands into his pockets, but that felt too confrontational. He took them back out, but that felt awkward. Ray had grown his hair out and wore it tied back in a messy bun, wavy tendrils escaping in the wind. Damian instinctively wanted to tuck them back behind Ray's ears.

"Hell of a drive from New York City, just for a conversation," Ray said. "Why didn't you call?"

"You changed your number."

Ray rolled his eyes. "Min still has my number. You could have gotten it from her."

He hadn't even thought of that. Why were Min and Ray still talking to each other and not to *him*? He was the connection between them, the common denominator. He'd assumed that they'd all lost touch at the same time, after he'd announced his book deal and they'd looked at him with betrayal instead of excitement. "I've got a proposition for you," he said to Ray. "And I figured you'd be less likely to turn me down in person."

Ray huffed—not quite a scoff, but too annoyed to be a laugh. "Good to know you're still a manipulative shit."

There was a soft, emphatic "Dang" from one of the students. Ray blushed and sent a withering glare at the group.

"I guess I deserve that," Damian said quietly. He absolutely deserved that. Even now, he was playing to their audience, calculating how much hurt to allow into his voice and vigorously hating himself for it. He wanted to be a good person, but he wanted to do good work more. This documentary was good—ergo: all was fair.

"Come on, you've distracted them enough," Ray said. "Step into my office."

His office was, of course, his truck, and if the sight of it had been a punch to the gut, actually stepped into it was like getting reverse-suplexed into the past. Same threadbare fabric on the seats. Same clatter of coffee cups rolling around the passenger footwell. Same dusty dashboard, with the word BUTTS etched into the leather near the passenger window—a gift from one of Ray's nephews. Ray had attempted to turn it into the word BURTS, supposedly in honor of Reynolds and Kwouk, but with meager success.

It was horrible. Damian only liked the past when it was a minimum of six hundred years old.

"The good old Buttsmobile," he said.

"It's the Burtsmobile, damn it," Ray muttered. "What's your proposition?"

"The Smithsonian wants to make a documentary about *ossicarminis*."

"Adapt your book, you mean?"

"Not just the book," Damian said. "They optioned it as an actual documentary about *ossicarminis*, finding and identifying them, the whole thing with NEOCO." He wasn't going to go into the Space Weasels. He could really only have one crisis of conscience at a time.

"And what happened after? Our falling-out? Or only the part of the story that makes you look good?" Ray asked. He'd always been blunt. Damian used to like that about him.

"Is that what you call it?" Damian asked, honestly interested. "A falling-out?"

Ray shrugged. "That's what other people call it when they're trying to ask me what happened."

"Falling-out," Damian said again, testing the words. Like it was natural, something to do with gravity, rather than two stubborn assholes roleplaying an unstoppable force meeting an immovable object.

"I told them I wouldn't do it without you and Min," Damian said. It wasn't quite a lie; assuring Annika that Ray and Min would definitely sign onto the project was basically the same thing. "The two of you *are* the story. More than me. I just got lucky by falling in a cave."

"*Ossicarminis* is the story," Ray said. "I—I don't—"

Damian waited him out, toying with the iron pendant his mother had made him in a smithing class. She said it was a fish, but it looked more like a frying pan.

"I don't want to rehash the whole fucking thing, man," Ray said eventually. A nice blush was spreading across his cheek. "Not what happened between us. That stays off camera and in the past."

"I am one hundred percent okay with that," Damian said, and knew it was a lie as soon as he said it. He had fallen into a fast, consumptive love with this nerdy asshole and his terrible khakis, his probably lethal caffeine habit, and his utter disinterest in being tactful. Their so-called falling-out hadn't changed that. He had originally planned on avoiding Ray forever, but since talking with Amelia, he'd come around rapidly to the idea that this could be his second chance. Hence actually driving out into this godforsaken prairie infested with Elvis-themed restaurants. They'd wanted the same thing, after all: to spread the word about *ossicarminis*, to make people understand the gravity of this discovery. They had disagreed loudly and angrily on how to do that, and Ray had dumped him.

And then he'd grown out his hair, which just seemed unfair.

"You grew out your hair," Damian said, like a lovesick idiot.

Ray looked surprised, then ran a hand over it. "I told myself I would when I got tenure. When they couldn't fire me for looking 'unprofessional.'" The word dripped with sarcasm. "Not sure if that meant too gay or too Indian. The chair never specified. Both, probably."

"Jesus fuck," Damian said, appalled. "Well, I hear they're all mad as hell now."

"They're gonna *die* mad," Ray said, grinning.

The familiarity was a physical ache; Damian thought of the feeling of taking off his binder after a day of wear, stretching his shoulders back after hunching them for hours. It was unfair, it was exquisite, and it felt like pressing hard on a bruise that he'd successfully ignored for the past year and a half.

"So?" he asked. "Documentary?

Ray stared him down, his expression shifting to something a little wearier. "Of course I'll do it." Damian had enough time to feel profoundly, shockingly grateful, before Ray held up a finger and said, "If..."

Damian already knew what he was going to say, but it still made his gut roil to hear it.

"*If* we rebury the bones."

Part Two: Min

I'm Min-ji Hong. I'm a PhD candidate in linguistics at the University of Chicago. Damian Flores is one of my oldest friends, which is presumably why I got dragged into this instead of, like, an established scholar? He probably knew I wouldn't try to steal the research out from under him.

How did I meet Damian? We went to summer camp together for gender non-conforming teens. We were some of the only non-white kids there, and we were both hyperactive science nerds. I was in Rivera Cabin, he was in Feinberg. We teamed up for some epic pranks on the bitches in Jenner after they called our scholarship cabins ghetto. We kept each other going through high school and college, but we lost touch a little once I started my PhD, and he went to work as a full-time activist.

My research is about writing systems. I focus on logographic systems, which...wait. It's going to take me a second translate this out of academic bullshit jargon. I've been ass-deep in dissertation revisions for weeks. So. Logographic writing systems use written characters to represent words, phrases, or ideas, as opposed to sounds. Characters in Latin alphabets refer to consonants and vowels, whereas Japanese kanji refer to concepts, for example. There are almost always some phonograms or phonetic complements, at least in complete writing systems, which, let's be clear, the ossicarmin script is not. Complete writing systems can be used to visually represent, in full, verbal communication. We only have the small sample size from this one group, but in my opinion—

Let me rephrase that, since I'm ABD and I've been waiting to claim this.

*In my **expert opinion**, ossicarminis didn't have a complete writing system. What they had is similar to what we see in some of the earlier Neolithic writing systems: pictograms on the edge of abstraction, carved into a set of bones. There's no way of translating it. There's no Rosetta Stone, which is a real tragedy. Still, calling the texts "oracle bones" is… well, it sounds more badass than "textual artifacts," but it's a total misnomer. They could be, like, receipts. The fact that they were found in a burial site doesn't necessarily mean they're the prehistoric weasel Bible. I have my own theories on what they are, but I'm saving those for **my** book.*

Before all this crap happened, I mostly focused on Anatolian protowriting systems. Now it's just the ossicarmin scripts. What else are you going to do when an entirely new writing system that was created by giant weasels or whatever is literally handed to you? Publish or perish, motherfucker. I've got this shit locked.

Huh? I was swearing? Sorry. I'll try harder.

***

She'd expected a nameless driver, but it was Ray waiting for her at baggage claim in San Francisco, tall and smiling and dressed in his signature ugly professor clothes. Min broke into a pleased smile, forgetting the cramped flight, the overwhelming feeling of being forced into close quarters with humanity after weeks of marinating in her own solitude.

"Mom says hi," Min said after they hugged. "And to tell you not to sleep with Damian."

"Sure, okay, tell her hi back, and to please never talk about my sex life again."

"No promises," Min replied. Mom had put it a little bit more nicely than that—she'd couched it in terms of unfinished business and looking for love in all the wrong places—but it was easy to make Ray blush. Min hadn't had the chance to do it in a while.

Ray held his hand out for her luggage, one of those old-fashioned gestures that gave her a little thrill of gender affirmation. Ray had always done chivalrous crap like that, which Min not-so-secretly loved because she was so rarely on the receiving end of it, a little too tall and sharp-featured to pass as cis.

She kept hold of her carry-on, though, and the little wooden box containing the oracle bones. The edges of it dug into her ribs, a sharp reminder of all that she hadn't told Ray.

"I probably would have backed out if you hadn't come," Ray said as they walked out into the muted California sunlight, "but I am really thankful you're here. You're the only one who knows who to keep Damian in line."

"It's practice," Min said. "I've been building up a tolerance for his brand of bullshit since I was fourteen."

It wasn't that she didn't love Damian—she did. She loved him as surely and deeply as she loved the Tărtăria tablets and Harry Potter fanfiction, with an understanding that for all their wonders, they tended to inspire endless drama.

**

Annika Wagner-Smith had suggested that they meet in a Chinese buffet called Sun King. She was, as Damian had said, Miss Frizzle as a Gender Studies/Media professor. Her hair went up, her glasses were round and severe, and she seemed to be aggressively fond of both tweed and purple accessories. She apparently hadn't waited for them to arrive before grabbing a plate and filling it with a half-demolished mountain of imitation crab. Had she only eaten crab?

Annika stood up when Min and Ray approached, dislodging a couple of crab sticks that flopped down onto the table cloth. She was surrounded by an entourage of crew members, some of whom Min recognized from the Chicago shoots. She waved cautiously to Kamal, the hot assistant director, and he waved back.

"Welcome, Ms. Hong, Mr. Walker," Annika said. She didn't seem to be speaking loudly, but her voice still carried across the room, as if she were bending the frequency of her voice to reach them. "We're still waiting on Damian, but please grab some plates."

Min side-eyed the buffet tables and the people being served. Mostly white families in tourist gear; she adjusted her expectations accordingly. She picked carefully through the food, selecting the least offensive-looking things, and grabbed Ray's arm when he looked thoughtfully at the salad bar.

"E. coli," she said. "Trust me, it's not worth it."

"You remember that I live in the middle of nowhere, right?" he said. "Last winter, the chair of the department decided to have our holiday party at Golden Corral."

She shuddered. "We're getting real food while we're here, right?" she asked. "I'm not coming out to San Francisco and not eating my weight in seafood."

"Can't you get fish in Chicago?"

Min's heart ached for Ray, so sad, so uncultured. "We're definitely getting brunch tomorrow."

Damian walked in right as they'd sat down to eat, and Annika repeated her strangely regal welcome. He waved off the offer of food, mentioning a late lunch, and satisfied himself with some green tea instead. He and Ray nodded politely to each other, sat on opposite sides of the table, and spent the rest of dinner furtively staring at each other. Min regretted relaying her mother's urge of abstinence to Ray; she hadn't realized how damn awkward things were between them already.

She ended up talking to Kamal, who had grown up on the South Side; they talked shit about the terrified suburban white students who walked in packs through Hyde Park until they realized that it wasn't actually the war zone everyone north of Roosevelt seemed to believe. She surreptitiously watched Annika go to the buffet no less than five more times, each time bringing back a plate piled high with only one kind of food: chicken wings, spring rolls, steamed vegetables, crab rangoon, pork dumplings. Each time, she steadily and single-mindedly worked her way through the plate until it was clear.

"I know, it's hard to look away," Kamal said.

"I don't know if I'm impressed or terrified."

Kamal sipped his Tsingtao. "Annika has that effect on people. I'm like, sixty percent sure it's on purpose?"

Annika went back to the buffet one last time, but returned only with a small plate of pudding. She set it down among the debris of her meal and the drift of wadded-up napkins, then clinked her spoon against her pudding bowl until everyone fell silent.

"Thank you all for coming. I am so happy to be here. So happy. So, so incredibly happy." She gazed around the table, making forcible eye contact with every person there. "I want to extend a special welcome to our three experts: Mister Damian Flores, and Doctors Hong and Walker."

Min momentarily felt the need to correct her—a long habit, since she'd been working on her PhD for six and a half goddamn years—but decided to let it pass. Fuck it.

"Kamal will be sending out the shooting schedule tonight. We're going to be based in San Francisco this week with segments at the

San Francisco Zoo, a wildlife rehabilitation center, and the natural history museum. Next week, we'll be in Nebraska, with reenactments at the site."

"What's this about a zoo?" Min asked Kamal.

He nodded. "We're going to get one or two of you into an otter habitat while someone else visits the wolverines."

Min turned to him with a steely look in her eye. She laid her hand firmly on his arm, and he glanced down at it curiously.

"I call dibs," she said solemnly, pressing her nails lightly against his skin. "The otters are *mine*."

He smiled, obviously terrified. "That's cool. I'll let Annika know."

***

Did you not hear me when I introduced myself? I'm a linguist. I study writing systems. I don't give a fuck who would win in a fight. Not unless some ossicarminis decided to make an epic poem out of it.

Which...huh. Maybe that's what specimen 6 is.

***

They took Damian to the otter exhibit as well. She'd hoped she'd be able to go by herself, but going with Damian was the next best thing. She loved Ray, she did, but Ray was not susceptible to cuteness the way that she and Damian were. He would have stood there and sighed, and looked sad that the animals were in a zoo. And sure, yeah, zoos were evil, but Min got to hold a baby sea otter.

His name was Tufts. He legit sounded like a dog's squeaky toy. He was *fuzzy.*

"Ugh, his little *hands*." Min was broken.

"His flesh-tearing little *teeth*," Damian cooed.

"Hey, we were hoping to get some, like, science out of you guys?" Kamal said.

"Can't science," Damian said. "Too fuzzy."

Tufts the orphaned otter sneezed, and Min burst into tears.

"Okay, maybe we'll talk to some of the zookeepers," Kamal sighed.

"I am so thankful for testosterone," Damian said. "Otherwise I would be crying too."

"I know I said I'd only do this for the money," Min said, wiping her eyes on her shirt. "But if you had told me I'd be able to feed a baby otter fish giblets, I would have done it for free."

Damian whispered, "Oh my god. He pooped on me, and I don't even care. It smells disgusting, but I still want to cuddle him."

They did manage to do a half-serious interview later in the day, though they had to find Damian a different shirt first, free of otter feces.

"There's a lot that fossil records leave out," Damian said. "We have enough information to form theories but never prove them. We can't know, for instance, how *ossicarminis* took care of its young. Or its elderly. We know that they lived near freshwater, but we don't know the size of their bands."

"Groups of otters are called *romps*, actually," Min said, interrupting. She'd looked it up before coming here.

Damian gave her a look—she really hoped that glare made it onto the final reel. "We're still debating whether they're more closely related to otters or wolverines."

"Biologists like Ray are still debating that." Min shifted back in her seat. "We're also trying to answer other questions. What did *ossicarminis* think about? What did they fear? When they walked out into the night and looked up at the stars, what did they see?" Min was literally quoting from her dissertation at this point, but it sounded good, so she kept going. "What did the universe look like from their point of view?"

"We have so many questions," Damian said. "And so few answers. But that's life, isn't it? We let inertia carry us into a future with a—a shady flashlight that's going dim. We can barely understand where we've come from, and where our choices have led us, but we keep groping forward, trying to find a way out of the mess we've made."

There was a long moment of silence, before Min cleared her throat and said delicately, "You got a little off track there."

Damian was staring at a spot on the floor. "Yeah, I did," he said.

Min shot Kamal a look and said, "Could you get us some water? Water seems like a good idea right now."

Kamal nodded at one of the other crew members, who scurried off. Min leaned forward. "Okay, Damian—"

He held up a hand. "I know, this is really shitty timing."

"It is, yep."

"But holy shit, it's like I stopped and *realized*. How deeply and seriously up my own ass I've been."

They obviously weren't going to circumvent this. She leaned back in her chair and braced herself for a tirade about his feelings for Ray, and Ray's stubborn refusal to forgive him, and how Ray's long hair was a personal attack on Damian's weak, gay heart. Maybe Kamal could get one of his underlings to fetch her some booze instead.

Damian looked at her searchingly. "I am so sorry," he said.

Min stared at him. "Wait, what?"

"I wrote the book without you. *Oracle Bones.* I quoted from you so much—hell, there are two chapters where I'm basically paraphrasing your preliminary findings."

"Damian!" Min said sharply. "What are you talking about?"

"Jesus, Min, I'm trying to apologize," Damian said. "I should have made you a co-author for *Oracle Bones*, not just quoted you. Ray, too, obviously, but you're my oldest friend. And it was shitty."

"If you were actually my friend, you'd stop trying to have this conversation with me *in public*, when we are *on camera*."

Sure, she'd been stung by the news that Damian had found a publisher for a manuscript about finding *ossicarminis*. After all that they'd been through together—not only facing a bunch of asswipes from the Nebraska Energy and Oil Commission, but like, *all of it*. All the nights the three of them had spent in drafty tents, working by hand-wound lanterns, making supply runs into Chadron, the only nearby town with a grocery store that also sold liquor. They'd been isolated out there, and every night she'd felt the clock ticking away toward the deadline that the Commission had set before they would start digging. It had been hard enough going back to Chicago, back to her studies on Anatolian scripts. She'd lasted a week before telling her advisor that she was tossing her previous work and going all in on the *ossicarminis* script. Nobody had understood. It had driven her to drink, the way that the world absorbed the discovery of *ossicarminis* like a penny sinking into a pool of Jell-O. At one point, she considered taking out a full-page ad in the *Sun-Times* that said "INTELLIGENT PREHISTORIC MUSTELIDS ARE MORE IMPORTANT THAN THE CUBS' CHANCES IN THE PENNANT OR LUWIAN HIEROGLYPHS."

And *then* the news that Damian was publishing a book. By himself. *The* book: the authoritative text about the discovery of the only non-hominid species with a written language. Min had heard the phrase *publish or perish* nearly every day since she matriculated, and that news slid between her ribs like a knife. Damian would publish and leave them to perish.

Leave *her*, rather. At least Ray had tenure, even if it was at a podunk state college in fucking Kansas.

She and Damian stared at each other for a long minute, until Kamal cleared his throat and said quietly, "You should hug."

Min had actually managed to forget he was there. "Are you fucking recording this?" she asked.

He raised his eyebrows. "I needed something better than the two of you crying over otters."

"I don't fucking *want* to hug him," Min said. She was somehow angrier than she'd been at the start of all this.

"You could hit him instead?" Kamal suggested. "That would also be great."

"Fight, fight, fight," the boom operator chanted softly.

***

Min had a weird relationship with museums. As a historical linguist, she needed archives to keep textual artifacts that would allow her to track the evolution of language, symbol, and meaning, and the interactions between the three. As someone who actually knew something about the history of museums, though, she couldn't go into one without feeling a twinge of guilt. Canons exclusively comprised of white cis men, the centering of the colonial gaze, cultural appropriation—she could probably write an entire essay about it, and maybe she would, when the sight of her laptop stopped giving her hives. But you could say nearly all the same things about higher education, and that hadn't stopped her from tossing herself into the shark-infested waters of academia nearly a decade ago.

Still, she felt a weird glow of pride at the actual *ossicarminis* exhibit at the Kimball Museum. She and Damian had been there at the opening. Ray had been invited but, as he told her later, didn't reply; he had, in fact, used the invitation to scoop up his neighbor's dog's shit.

("Ray, the invitation was emailed."

"I know. I printed it out just for the occasion.")

The room was wide and well-lit, with the two skeletons encased in glass; it reminded her a little bit of the mausoleums and crystal coffins where the bodies of Ho Chi Minh and Mao Zedong rested. Museum-goers filed past the cases where the two skeletons lay, having been expertly articulated and laid out in their original positions from the cave. The larger skeleton, with a heavy skull and long tail, curled around the smaller. The bones were flawless, with no obvious trauma, almost as if they'd both died in their sleep.

Min liked to joke that she didn't really have a heart—grad school had chewed it up until there was nothing left but gristle. Still, the sight of the two skeletons hit her on some deep, complicated maternal level; there was something so protective about the stance, so loving. If they had, as Ray believed, been intentionally buried in that cave, it was both easy and heart-destroying to imagine a group of mourning *ossicarminis* arranging the adult around the child to protect it in the afterlife.

A group of schoolkids came through, tailed by a couple of exhausted chaperones. They ran up to the glass coffin and smeared greasy fingerprints all over it, shouting over each other. Min took a couple steps back, maternal moment obliterated by the sticky reality of real children. None of them even looked at the panels about the discovery or the writing. The room was utter chaos for a few minutes, until the kids got bored and bounded off to the next exhibit. They were followed by another actor in a neon-green spandex suit, playing the part of an *ossicarminis*.

"Okay, okay, yes," Annika said loudly, following him with the camera. "Approach them like they are your relatives. Your ancestors. Hero-gods from another age. Someone you have never set eyes on, but still have deep reverence and love for."

The actor laid his green-gloved hands reverently on the glass.

"Put your face on the glass," she said, and the actor touched his forehead gently to the case. "No! No! This is not a funeral! You're a rascal and you are blowing raspberries at the past!"

Min frowned, but the actor didn't seem to mind the sudden change of mood. He smashed his cheeks against the glass and blew a raspberry. Min shuddered, thinking of how many various orifices the kids had probably put their fingers in before touching the glass. She moved on to look at the large wall panel display of the oracles—goddamn it, the *textual artifacts*. It had always annoyed her that the texts were literally sidelined in the exhibit, flat and static against the wall. Most of the visitors ignored them in favor of the skeletons.

A metaphor for her research if there ever was one.

The next shoot took place in a fancy museum conference room, with a stone wall with real moss growing out of it. This was the three-way interview that Min had, with equal anticipation and dread, been looking forward to.

It was not going terribly well. Ray was giving an extensive explanation of why he'd declined to go into the *ossicarminis* exhibit, both when it opened and during the current visit.

"I hate museums," said Ray. He had his arms crossed. "And I really hate natural history museums."

On Min's other side, Damian toyed with his necklace like he was thinking of strangling someone with it. His face was bright red, and he stared at the ground in a way that made Min think there were Kill Bill sirens going off in his head.

"Interesting," Annika said. "That seems at odds with your line of work."

"I like looking at bones, not putting them on display. Gawking at dead people is a terrible violation of their dignity, unless you don't think those people are human. Do you know how many of my ancestors' bones ended up in museums like this?" He gestured around them. "Or are still here, in some cases. We're counted among so-called natural history. You'll never see a pilgrim or a conquistador's skeleton in a place like this, because that's disturbing the dead. An

Indian? That's an educational opportunity. And I hate that the two *ossicarminis* skeletons are in here, too."

Annika nodded thoughtfully; she seemed to be doing her best Barbara Walters impression. Then she turned to Damian. "Would you like to respond to that?"

Damian took a deep breath, tucking the necklace back into his shirt.

"When I was a kid—"

"Oh, here we go," Ray muttered.

"*When I was a kid,*" he repeated, glaring at Ray. "I grew up in Florida. I was the strange, nerdy kid that nobody wanted to talk to, because I generally wanted to talk about things like the body segments of insects or how cool Carl Sagan was. I had two friends, and they were PBS and the Frost Museum of Science. Museums were the only place where I felt like all of my interests were normal. Like *I* was normal."

Min waited to see if he'd add to that, explain the weight of "normality" to a trans kid. Min watched him struggle with it, and in the end, decide against it. She couldn't blame him; she wasn't in a rush to out herself on camera either. Some things you kept for yourself or for people like you.

"Museums are places where kids—and adults!—encounter science and history at a hands-on level. It's where they first make contact with new knowledge and new ideas, and sometimes the only place where they can do that outside of a classroom. I would never have been inspired to study environmental science or archeology if my interest hadn't been piqued in that museum. *Ossicarminis* is one of the most groundbreaking discoveries of the century, and the exhibit ensures that people don't forget that."

"Then put replicas out!" Ray said. "Most of the people who come through won't know the difference, or care. There's no reason that the real bones of *real people* should be displayed."

"Doctor Walker, do you consider *ossicarminis* to be, as you said, 'real people'? Human, in a way?"

Ray snorted. "They were buried. Their bodies were taken care of and buried together so they wouldn't be alone. I can't think of anything more human than that."

"And I don't disagree," Damian said. "They were absolutely people. But we have a duty to the *public*—"

"To make sure your name is plastered all over everything? What, is your Wikipedia entry not *big enough* for you?"

Damian stared at him. "Was that a dick reference?"

Min cleared her throat. "Height joke, I think." At Damian's wounded stare, she added, "Come on, your Napoleon complex is well-documented."

Ray barked out a laugh.

Damian looked from her to Ray and back again. "Wow, fuck the pair of you."

"Doctor Hong, did you have an opinion on the subject of museums?" Annika asked, obviously desperate to get back on topic.

"Just that you should never go on a date in one," she said.

There was a moment of silence. "Maybe we should take a break," said Annika.

She gestured to Kamal, who said, "That's a cut!" The cameraman turned the camera off, and the boom operator relaxed with a soft groan. "We're going to take five."

Annika wandered away, and the crew followed. Kamal said, "Y'all want coffee or anything? Water?"

Min and Ray nodded to the offer of caffeine, while Damian sat silently, in a full-blown snit now. She recognized all the signs. Kamal left them alone to their tense, angry silence.

"So museums are bad," Damian said, his tone ice-cold and casual. "What's your stance on the individual possession of sacred artifacts?"

Min, too late, remembered that Damian was actually really insecure about his height. It was one of those soft spots that you learned to never poke, not even—or maybe especially not—as a joke. Damian had learned how to fight from his mother, partly to spit in the eye of Latin machismo, partly because it was terrifying effective. Min had seen him exact swift, decisive revenge on presumptuous assholes who never believed the cheerful guy a full head shorter than them would throw down with all the rage of an auntie on a Miami street corner. She should have remembered the pranks on the bitches in Jenner cabin.

"What are you talking about?" Ray said.

"Say, for instance, you wanted a closer look at the only physical evidence ever recorded of non-human writing systems. So you stole it from a university archive and kept it in your filthy-ass apartment. On the goddamn mantle. In *direct sunlight*." Damian looked directly at Min. "And then kept it there for more than a year because, fuck it, something about grubby undergrads not appreciating it."

Ray leaned forward and looked at her too. Min desperately wished, at any point in her life, that she had effectively learned how to lie. It always came so easily to Damian. But no, she'd inherited her mother's compulsion to overshare.

"Min," Ray said urgently. "Is this for real?"

This must be the disappointed face that Damian had warned her about.

She couldn't think of a single thing to say to him. Maybe she could have with enough time, but he didn't wait. He stood up, grabbed his jacket from the back of the chair, and stalked off.

"Holy fuck," she whispered.

"Welcome to the hell," said Damian, leaning back in his seat. "Glad you could join me here."

***

I see Ray's point. I do. I think that humans right now, most of us anyway, think of the Earth as a big piggy bank that we can keep pulling stuff out of. And yeah, we need to eat, we need to keep civilization running, we need to at least ensure that our species can do more than simply survive, and we need resources to do that. Knowledge serves a deeper purpose than, like, accumulating a series of initials after your name. Not that you'd fucking know it if you went to grad school. Jesus.

What was I talking about?

*Oh right. Yeah. Both sides. Look, I love Damian, but I don't love his ambitions. And I love Ray but not his **lack** of ambitions, you know? And I really love the oracle bones, even though that name is garbage and a total rip-off.*

But we need to stop borrowing against the future. And the past, too. It belongs to all of us. I guess that means that it also belongs to them, right? To ossicarminis.

Huh.

Shit.

***

Alone in her hotel room, Min pulled out the oracle bones.

It was such a misnomer, honestly. She had side-eyed the hell out of Damian when he'd started calling them that, and the two of them had eventually gotten into the kind of knock-down shouting match that can only happen between stubborn academics when they're drunk on too much cheap wine from a gas station. She hadn't wanted to put labels on the *ossicarminis* script; calling them *oracles* infused them with a cultural value that they might not have had. Not that it made them less important, which Damian should have known. He had a degree in archeology, and had, more than once, waxed poetic about the information one could glean from a prehistoric garbage heap. He had done an entire TEDx talk about it, proof that he was a self-aggrandizing dork even before the book deal. The bones didn't need to be pseudo-religious artifacts in order to be one of the most important discoveries of the twentieth century. (Which was basically a summary of her third chapter.)

"But we need people to *pay attention*," Damian had slurred. "We need to give them a reason to *care*, otherwise this whole fuckin' site is gonna be dug up and turned into a fuckin' wasteland. If not now, then someday."

The bones were heavy in her hand. The marks into the bone matched the relative angle and depth of the claws found on the skeleton. They'd smeared them with an organic dye, some cousin to a walnut, which meant they'd been tool users, though of a different sort to humans. They probably hadn't used stone tools, since they hadn't needed to.

But they'd had language. And they had thought about time.

That was the real reason writing evolved: the need for some semblance of permanence. An acknowledgement that words couldn't last and memory was fallible. *Ossicarminis* had their own stories, and they'd wanted them to be preserved for the future.

Min sorted through the bones and looked at specimen three. Ray had identified it as belonging to the metatarsals of some giant-ass monster bird—she could recite whole passages of the *Aeneid* in the original Latin, but she could never remember the proper names of that species—and the marks were scrawled with what she believed to be a different hand than the other specimens, and possibly at a later date. The symbols were further into abstraction, more stylized, surer than on the other bones. Many of the symbols were naturalistic, though you had to kind of squint and shrug to interpret them. A fern, a fish, a bird in the sky, arrangements of circles and chevrons.

They were more ordered here, written in columns along the tibia. She smiled, imagining an industrious *ossicarminis* scribe writing down the epic battle between a band—no, a *romp*—of its fellows and a saber-toothed cat. And sure, it was a stupid question, but it was easy to imagine that those sickle shapes up at the top referred to *Smilodon's* teeth, and the collection of lines symbolized the number of brave *ossicarminis* that took it out.

It was just as likely that the bones really were a receipt for the collection of the shiny stones that *ossicarminis* had collected. Stories of battles had been preserved by word of mouth and memory long before anyone bothered writing them down. The oldest cuneiform tablets were records of economic transactions, the trade of cattle and wheat, not heroic epics. Still, Min understood the desire to preserve the odd tales of triumph. There were never enough.

Min rubbed her fingers over the sickle-shaped gouges. Damian would scream at her for not wearing gloves. Ray would give her another one of those devastating disappointed looks. She sighed and put the oracle bone back in the box.

Google Maps led her to the closest liquor store to the motel, and she bought the cheapest box of wine on the shelf. Not even because she was broke—Annika had assured them that the Smithsonian network would reimburse them for incidentals. But there was something to be said for tradition.

"Okay, so listen," Min said when Damian opened the door. "I wasn't mad at you. I really wasn't."

Damian looked down the hallway, then opened his door the rest of the way. "Are we really doing this now?"

Min shouldered past him. "I brought booze. Figured if we were gonna get into this shit, we weren't gonna do it sober."

She gave him the box of White Zinfandel and sat down on the bed.

"Wow. Should we completely give up on dignity and drink it out of plastic cups?"

"Whatever," Min said. "We're talking about feelings, which is undignified enough." She accepted her cup of wine, drank half of it, grimaced, then drank the rest.

"So you weren't mad?" Damian prompted.

"I wasn't," Min said. "Until you apologized at the zoo. Then I got all pissed off because, because...motherfucker, you really did ditch my ass by the side of the road once you got what you needed from me. And I never really had any time to be resentful of that because I got sucked into a vortex of having to do all this research myself. But now, I'm...holy shit, I'm so fucking mad at you."

"I—"

"And your shitty science! Like the fact that you railroaded us into calling them oracle bones instead of *literally anything else.* Did you even know that oracle bones are already a thing in linguistic history?"

"I said I was sorry," Damian said. His voice did that soft hurt thing, which annoyed her even more. Jesus, she wasn't some simpering suburban housewife at a fundraiser. She wasn't *Ray.* She wasn't gonna fall for that.

"So what?" she said. "That doesn't mean you get to circumvent me being pissed off at you. I was just too busy with other shit for the last year and a half."

She held up her empty cup. Damian actually rolled his eyes before taking it, refilling it, and handing it back. She sipped this cup more slowly, though not with any more enjoyment.

"And you know what the worst thing is?" she said. "I actually think you did the right thing, at least for a given value of 'right.'"

Damian moaned and lay down on the other side of the bed. "God, fucking academics. I hate the way you talk."

"At least I don't snitch on my friends." She threw a pillow at him.

Damian glared at her. "Look, I really don't want to fight with you."

She threw another pillow, harder this time. "Why not? It would probably be healthy for us to work out our mutual resentment. My mom is always talking about healthy ways of resolving conflict."

He threw the pillow back at her, and it caught her right in the face as she was about to take a sip of the terrible wine. White Zinfandel went up her nose, into her eyes, and splashed across the bed.

"You *fuck!*" Min shouted, and launched herself at him.

The weird thing was, it actually *did* feel healthy. Min had spent the last six years navigating the delicate politics of the linguistics department and the university, compounded by the fact that she was a woman of color and trans. She'd had to remain perfectly poised even while literally losing her hair from the stress, doing research that everybody half-believed was a hoax. She was overdue for an utter shitfit, and Damian—well, Damian wasn't the department chair who had belittled her research or that scumbag Jerome who stole her original topic, and he definitely wasn't that visiting professor who offered her an underpaid research assistanceship while telling her she was "so intriguingly exotic." (She'd turned him down, but it took hours before she could reply with anything besides "Fuck you you racist sexist shitfuck.")

Damian wasn't the reason grad school was a miserable slog, but he had ditched her and made her suffer through it alone, and wow, apparently she had developed abandonment issues along the way.

"I missed you, you asshole!" she said, and punched him in the ribs. Not very hard; she didn't actually know how to punch.

"Bitch!" Damian shouted. "I missed you too!" He managed to shove her off for a brief moment, but she grabbed onto his legs before he could flee. This was great. It was like being back at Camp Transcendent, at the end-of-summer mud wrestling competition. Only with more rug burn, and Damian wasn't actually fighting back.

Min managed to get in a few more hits before they were interrupted by a pounding at the door.

"Oh shit," Damian said. They both looked around the room. They'd managed to knock over a standing lamp and the desk chair. The room stank of sour wine.

They tried to disentangle themselves, but the door opened before they could. Ray's aura of seething disappointment preceded him into the room. He seemed to suck the post-fight endorphins right out of Min's brain.

"What the fuck are you two doing?" he asked.

Damian pointed at her. "She absolutely started it."

"To be fair," Min said, trying to get her hair back in some kind of order. "I just finished writing my dissertation, so some kind of break with reality was inevitable."

Ray, bless him, shrugged and said, "That makes sense."

Min ignored him and spoke to Kamal, who was lingering in the doorway, filming. "You! Turn the camera off."

Then she turned to Ray. "What are you doing here? And why do you have a key to Damian's room?"

Ray looked down at his hand, which still clutched the plastic keycard. Damian's cheeks were pink and his eyes looked hopeful. Ew.

"That's... a complicated question," he said.

"I slipped it to him at the bar last night," Damian offered. "Not actually that complicated. Does this mean you forgive me?"

"Both of us?" Min added, because she was weak and hated when people were mad at her.

"I can't believe you." Ray shifted his gaze to include Min as well. "It's not about forgiveness, and believe it or not, it's not about you, your egos, or your goddamn feelings!"

"So you're still mad," Damian said.

Ray threw the plastic room key on the floor. "I'm going back to Kansas. Min, don't you dare tell your mom about this."

"Wait, why the hell would you tell your *mom*?" Damian cried as Ray slammed the door.

Thank god the boxed wine was intact.

***

Do I think ossicarminis went to space? Like, instead of becoming extinct?

Sure. Why the fuck not. God knows I'm tempted to yeet myself into the void half the time. Better than paying back student loans.

***

The morning after: offensively sunny.

Ray's phone: straight to voicemail.

Min's hangover: vicious.

The only comfort she took at all was that Damian's appeared to be equally terrible.

"You look fucking awful," she told him. She had, at some point, decided that she was too drunk to make it back to her own room, and had fallen asleep on the other side of the king-sized bed.

"Probably not as awful as I feel," he said miserably. He ran his hand through his patchy beard and groaned. "I'm gonna puke and see if that makes me feel better."

Min hoped, with sincere viciousness, that *ossicarminis* went extinct before they discovered alcohol. If she could erase ten thousand years or more of human history and tell those assholes in the Fertile Crescent to put down those fucking grapes, she would.

Damian locked himself into the bathroom while Min turned on the TV, flipping through channels with the volume turned up as loud as her headache would allow. They had thoroughly destroyed Damian's room: the lamp was still overturned, and empty bottles, a pile of chip bags, and a half-finished cheese plate crowded the tables and floor by the bed. Had they ordered a cheese plate? No wonder Damian was upchucking. Dumbass was lactose intolerant, but conveniently forgot that whenever cheese was involved.

She fumbled for the phone and dialed the front desk. "Do you all have room service?" The Smithsonian was on the hook for all their room charges, she was pretty sure. Even if they weren't, it was Damian's room, and he owed her. She vaguely remembered him saying so last night, with that sincerity that only the extremely inebriated could manage.

She doubled her side order of bacon, then begrudgingly ordered a plate for Damian as well. She had managed to work through most of her anger, but the resentment still lingered deep under her skin.

About fifteen minutes after the food arrived, Damian exited the bathroom with a towel wrapped around his waist, accompanied by a billow of steam. The shower and shave had improved his appearance, but he still looked distinctly miserable. At least until he caught sight of the containers of food.

"Oh, shit," Damian said. He sat down on the bed in his towel and snagged a piece of bacon. Bruises the exact shape and size of her fists dotted his torso, so she figured he'd earned it. Having consumed one plate of bacon and made a dent in the other, Min was feeling a little more charitable and a little less like living death. She pushed the Styrofoam container at him.

"Breakfast poutine," she explained. "French fries and eggs and some other shit. Avocados, because everything in the Bay Area has avocados. No cheese, because you're not allowed to puke anymore while I'm in range."

"If I weren't gay and you weren't my oldest friend, I would marry you so hard right now," Damian said, accepting the plate.

Min didn't argue. She felt herself relaxing in a way that she rarely felt able to, at least around other people, even as her esophagus burned with bile and her head pounded. Even as, she remembered, one of the most important people in both her and Damian's life was probably cursing the fact that he'd ever met either of them.

That was a problem for after coffee.

They ate in companionable silence, friendlier than any recent silence that Min could remember with Damian. He tended to talk, to burble like an overenthusiastic fountain. She had to talk louder to keep up, to own some of the space that he effortlessly occupied. It had been good practice for grad school, but she still resented it.

"So," Damian said. "You punched the shit out of me. Does that mean we're good now?"

She glared at him over the rim of her nearly empty coffee. "Maybe."

"What if I use my clout to get you a publisher for your dissertation?"

She glared harder at him. "Fuck you."

"Okay, so it would be Amelia's clout, and she'll probably want to sign you as a client herself, but like. The offer stands."

He waited as she finished off her coffee.

"Fine," she muttered. Part of her wanted to turn him down and do it all herself. Wasn't self-made success the best possible revenge? On the other hand, grad school had forced her to acknowledge that bootstrapping was a myth for white men embarrassed by their own privilege. She'd take a bribe of talking with an agent over the likelihood of having to adjunct at three different schools to pay her bills.

"Great!" he said, then winced. Good, Min thought. She was still too hungover for his normal levels of enthusiasm. "Now that that's settled, are you going to hit me if I change the subject to Ray?"

"I'm too tired to hit you again," Min admitted. Also, they should probably talk about Ray.

"So."

"So."

"We really fucked up."

Min resented being included in that, but it wasn't inaccurate. "Yeah, we did."

"And he's in the right." Damian drank his own coffee.

Min pushed her face into the pillows, remembering Ray's *et tu, Brute?* look of betrayal. "Ugh, *yes*. Yes, he's fucking right. What's your bright idea to fix all of this? He wants the skeletons and the oracles back in the cave, but—"

"But there's an entire mountain of paperwork that says San Francisco has the right to display the skeletons for the next three years, and the state of Nebraska ultimately owns them," Damian finished. "Trust me, I have been making *a lot* of calls. If it happens, it's going to take years."

"Can we steal them?" she asked blearily. "Like, hire a team of washed-up secret agents or something and pull off an art heist?" She paused. "A skeleton heist?"

"Yeah, I don't have that kind of money. And I don't know any former secret agents."

"And how would you know if you did?" she muttered.

"I'm just saying—" Damian started.

She pulled another pillow on top of her, hiding in it. "I *know*, okay, I fucking *know*—"

"—that we have already successfully stolen some of the things he wants to re-inter—"

"God *damn* it."

"—and could put them back in the cave, with nobody but us the wiser."

"Us and Ray."

"Of course."

Min sat up, knocking her pillow fortress to the floor. "This still makes us shitty people, you know. We're both doing what's right to get back in his good graces."

"The first part of that sentence is the part that matters," Damian said confidently, then sobered a little. "Okay, yeah, it's fucked up. But we can work on being better people later."

Part 3: Ray

My name is Raymond Walker. I'm a professor of biology at Emporia State University, in Kansas. Weird name for a town. I always thought it sounded like the name of a giant flea market.

Right, sorry. In the spring of 2017, I received this email asking me to lend my expertise on a dig in northwestern Nebraska. It was the middle of the semester, so I couldn't really leave. I wrote back, kind of turning the guy down, telling him I was busy. He keeps emailing, and the next thing I know, this guy is calling me, begging for a Skype meeting. I say yes, because...I don't know why. He was pushy, and he spelled my name wrong in the email, and the whole thing irritated me. I think I only agreed so I could tell him to fu—to screw off. But then he showed me the bones.

The skull first, and I thought, okay, fine, he needs me to confirm some fossils. I did my dissertation on North American megafauna, and I research—you guys probably aren't interested my actual research, are you? Only this stuff.

All right. So, Damian starts uploading all these pictures of the rest of the skeleton, and—you know how rare it is to find a complete fossil? Even fossils from recent epochs, it's always down to luck. There are so many ways that bones get destroyed. Time swallows them up. The earth swallows them up. Rivers bury them, earthquakes break them, animals eat them. You have basically every natural process working against you when you're looking for fossils. It's always luck. Damian's got good luck, I guess.

So, Damian shows me pictures of these bones, and I can see he's got two complete skeletons: an adult and a juvenile. And I started getting excited, because I'm a bone nerd. That's what my niece says. Two skeletons, almost complete, is a huge find.

And then Damian shows me this other set of bones, with markings on them. No. With words on them. They've been carved and dyed. Preliminary carbon dating on both the bones and the dye put them at three and a half million years old. And I'm thinking, even if this is a hoax, it's a damn impressive one.

And then Damian tells me that they're digging because the state is planning to sell the land off to a natural gas company, and they're going to frack the whole area. Ten minutes after that, I made some calls, packed up my car, and started driving north.

***

Ray had never thought of himself as histrionic, but Min and Damian apparently brought it out in him. He took a shuttle to the airport early that morning and, when it was obvious that changing his flight was more money than he could really spend on a dramatic gesture, rented a car. He'd lived his entire life on the high prairie, where a four-hour drive was routine and a ten-hour drive was a normal weekend trip. But three days on the road was a trial even for him.

Luckily he had cousins in Utah and Colorado who were willing to put him up, all his father's Lakota kin—he'd dropped contact with most of his white mother's family after they started posting MAGA memes on Facebook and yelling about Standing Rock being a liberal hoax. His dad's family weren't the kind of cousins you could reliably trace a blood connection to, but the kind who knew to ask after your grandma's diabetes and shared embarrassing stories about your uncles from back in the day.

"Where are you coming from again?" Cousin Anita in Fort Collins asked, between shoving a plate of reheated leftovers at him and scolding him for coming in so late.

"California. The Smithsonian's doing a documentary about the weasels."

She whistled, impressed. "Gonna be a movie star now too?" She grinned. "You got the face for it. You're *Bachelorette* material for sure."

They joked around as he finished eating her food. He had missed being teased, being taken not-so-seriously. It was one of the reasons he had kept in touch with Min; she always had time to take him down a peg or talk endless shit about the quagmire that was academia. It was one of the things he still missed about Damian. Everyone in Kansas was too polite, too soft with their ribbing. They kept all their meanness behind closed doors.

"How are those weasels doing?" Anita asked.

"Still intelligent and still dead," he answered. "Just like the last three million years."

Ray was a bit of a curiosity to the tangled extensions of his family. They teased him about living in Kansas, which they seemed to collectively regard as the only state potentially worse than South Dakota, or about his perpetual singlehood, but mostly about his brief fame as one of the guys who discovered some kind of smart weasel from a few million years ago.

None of the Lakota side of his family took the premise that an animal could have a rich, social, intelligent life as bullshit. None of them scoffed at a weasel having enough introspection to want to write things down. That all made sense. The only funny part of the whole thing was that he'd helped discover it—Frank Walker's youngest kid, the one who'd thrown up at the school recital and broke his nose trying to catch a fly ball during baseball practice.

But they respected that he'd gotten the state of Nebraska to back down from destroying a chunk of Pine Ridge. He still had cousins buying him beers for that one.

Maybe that was what brought him around on the whole stupid documentary. It *was* a good story, after all. A weird little collection of activists and nerds made a discovery, organized, and saved the land from being torn open and destroyed. It meant a lot, that his siblings' kids had a story like that to grow up with. *Ossicarminis*, in his mind, confirmed that the separation between animals and people wasn't an impermeable border. It was hand-shaking distance between neighbors. They were all tied together, hardly different than Ray and his far-flung cousins.

You didn't put your neighbors' bones on display in a museum for schoolchildren to gawk at. It was good to know that *ossicarminis* were here first, that such a people had existed. But they had been put in the ground with care and love, and that was where they should have remained.

He hadn't meant to let all of that out on camera, but…well. Maybe it was for the best. He'd told Damian he didn't want their whole *thing* to be part of the documentary, but he wasn't sure he knew how to separate the two. Damian had a good heart, but he was devoted to getting what he wanted. He mostly wanted good things— that was what had attracted Ray in the first place, along with the fact that Damian had biceps for days—but the stubbornness that made him an effective activist also made it impossible to argue with him. They hadn't had a falling-out so much as an inevitable collision.

The land east of Fort Collins stretched out comfortably, grasslands and ranches sprawling like animals at rest. Ray never felt more at home than in the high prairie, but he wished there was more to occupy his mind. With no scenery to distract him, there was nothing to do but click endlessly through radio stations and be bored.

Boredom wasn't all bad. Ray tended to take a long view, probably a side effect from thinking in terms of epochs and eras. There were about a billion years when life on Earth amounted to some extremely unexciting sludge. Boredom gave things time to ferment, to evolve...

Ray realized that he was basically reciting one of his freshmen microbiology lectures to himself and abandoned it.

Damian had been the opposite of boring ever since Ray met him, first as a voice talking too excitedly into the phone, then as a grainy, pixelated image holding up fossils to a shitty webcam, and then finally as a surprisingly short guy going toe-to-toe with the Nebraska energy commission. Damian had apparently called everyone that he knew to come down and swarm the site: a lot of environmental activists, a double handful of scientists, folks from local towns, and a large contingent from the Pine Ridge reservation. (Nobody Ray knew personally, but it only took ten minutes for them to figure out common acquaintances and that several of their fathers had served in the same infantry division in Vietnam.)

He stopped for gas just past the state border, after greeting the *Welcome to Kansas* sign with a "Hello to you too." He stretched as the gas pump clicked away.

He'd known, a day after meeting Damian, that he was exactly the sort of guy that made Ray weak in the knees. But Ray had never been a romantic—not when he was in his twenties, and not now that he was slouching through middle age. Damian had more passion and ambition than either of them knew what to do with, and an inability to sit still that made Ray itch. So he'd never expected anything long-term from Damian. Ray figured he'd be like a lot of other flings, the kind of attachment that came with a long lead rather than a short leash. That's what he'd hoped, at least.

They had celebrated long into the night when the state announced that it was holding off on developing the land due to its historical and scientific significance. Then the state officials announced they were loaning the skeletons to a museum. That was bad enough, but then Damian announced his book deal. Ray had caught the look of seething betrayal on Min's face, and felt something in him rear up defensively. Getting cut out of a project like that was like watching one of your own limbs getting lopped off.

The gas pump clicked off, knocking Ray off the carousel of memories he'd been going around on. He pulled the pump out of the car, replaced it, and went to get a bottle of Coke and some chips. He still had a long way to go.

***

Seriously? Holy crap. Please tell me you're going to animate a fight between Smilodon and a band of ossicarminis. There's no way that ever would have happened, but who cares, it would be awesome. For the record, my money's on ossicarminis. They were social animals and probably hunted in packs. And they were effective enough to have maybe brought down a Teratorn—

Of course they would fight together. Okay, we don't know that they hunted in packs, and their teeth definitely indicate omnivorous diets, so it's possible that most of their food was vegetal. But I believe, to the core of my being, that they would have fought together. It's possible they found a dead Teratorn and scavenged the bones, but it is way more badass to imagine them fighting together.

So yeah. They definitely could have taken out a sabertooth tiger. No problem, as long as they…as long as they stuck together.

***

There were six voicemails and seventeen missed calls on his phone by the time he got back to his little house in Emporia, and even more the next morning. All the voicemails were from people on the Smithsonian crew, up to and including Annika herself, reassuring him that it was completely understandable if he needed some time away from the shoot, but to please remember that he was still under contract, and to let the scheduler know immediately if he wouldn't be able to make it to Nebraska the following week. The "or else, motherfucker" was heavily implied.

The rest of the calls were from Min and Damian, who were both, of course, allergic to leaving messages.

He left them all hanging for another day, and spent the next day running the sort of mindless errands that he inevitably put off during the semester: changing light bulbs, cleaning out his truck, throwing out all of his students' homework that he'd meant to grade but hadn't. He tried to imagine Min or Damian being happy with the kind of life he'd carved out for himself and knew they couldn't. They had both joked about his relative lack of ambition, teaching in a small town in Kansas; he didn't have the heart to tell them that for most of his students, and for him, Emporia was relatively cosmopolitan. Hell, he was still one of the success stories in his family and around the Rosebud reservation, a weapon his siblings used to bludgeon the importance of education into their kids' heads. It annoyed him that Min and Damian saw where he was and thought he'd settled for less than he deserved.

He called the producers back first, assuring them that yes, he'd be in Nebraska next week, and yes, he was very sorry for running out, it wouldn't happen again. After that, he debated between calling Min or Damian back, and realized that if he actually wanted to communicate with either of them, texting would probably work better.

Dinner next week? He sent to Min. *I'll be in Omaha on Thursday.*

The answer was immediate. *Yes please.* It was followed by one of those interminable ellipses as she typed an apparent novel into the message box. But all that came through, eight minutes later, was *We have a lot to talk about.*

He sent a thumbs up emojo, or whatever they were called.

***

The first day of shooting in Nebraska wasn't, in fact, at the dig site, but at a studio in Omaha. They had made a to-scale model of the cave, an almost perfect replica. The two skeletons were in the center of a faux-dirt floor, illuminated by an ethereal play of light and shadow. It was almost more real than his actual memories. The rest of it felt wrong: too hot from the lights and dry, noisy from all the bodies moving through the space, calling out to each other, smelling like wood dust and paint instead of wet dirt. It was disorienting, like being in two places at once.

"Doctor Walker!" Annika Wagner-Smith said, after an assistant had abandoned him in the middle of the chaos. He braced himself for an uncomfortable amount of eye contact, but this time, it was the prolonged handshake that threw him off.

"I am so happy you made it," she said, and her sincerity was like a brick wall crashing down around him. "So, so, very, *very* happy you are here."

"Ah, same, thanks." He liked her, he did. At least she was serious about this project. But having that seriousness aimed in his direction was intimidating.

"I want you to know that we really appreciate your perspective," she said. "I understand that emotions run high during shooting—"

"Yeah, sorry about—"

She squeezed the hand that she was *still* holding. "You should never apologize for an authentic expression of the self."

"Just let us get it on camera next time," Kamal muttered.

It took him a second to translate that into words he could understand: dramatic shitfits were acceptable, as long as they were recorded for posterity.

Annika finally let him go, and he self-consciously stuck both hands in his jacket pockets, lest she try to grab them again.

They conducted his main interview in the fake cave, as well as shooting a bunch of shots of him examining the prop skeletons, pretending to scrape away the dirt and soft claystone in which they'd been buried. The props looked extremely realistic, but felt rubbery and hollow—which of course they were. Ray could appreciate the artistry, and the metaphor, at work.

The interview was surprisingly enjoyable; some of the questions were tiresome, but most were at least entertaining. Hell, even the crackpot stuff made him laugh. Space weasels? It was stupid as hell, but Ray liked to imagine his sisters' kids watching the documentary and getting a kick out of that. Annika showed him some of the conceptual art, and Ray asked for a copy to hang in his office.

Then she threw a genuine curveball at him. He should have expected it.

"Would you mind telling us what Mister Flores and Doctor Hong said in San Francisco that made you so upset?" She said it so casually, like it was a natural follow-up to parasocial relationships in mammals.

Damn. Ray took a sip of coffee to buy some time to think. He didn't want Min to get in trouble, and god knew she'd be in deep shit if her school found out she'd switched the real things with the replicas. Damian's vindictiveness hadn't extended to saying anything on camera; he'd only wanted to snitch on her to Ray.

"Sorry, this is, uh," Ray muttered. He ran a hand through his hair again. "I don't know if I…"

What would Damian do in this circumstance, Ray thought desperately. He'd lie his ass off, right? No, he'd tell enough of the truth so nobody knew his true intentions.

"Damian and I were…together," he blurted. Min was going to owe him *so fucking bad* for this. At least he couldn't be fired for being queer in Kansas anymore, and he'd already gotten tenure.

Annika, to her credit, didn't bat an eye at the admission. Kamal, however, grinned like a cat that had just spotted a broken-winged canary.

"Together?" Annika prompted.

"Uh. Yeah. Romantically." That didn't seem entirely accurate, but there probably wasn't a word in English for how he felt about Damian, then or now. "We didn't end on the best terms."

"How so?"

"I think the exact phrase I used was 'egotistical, fame-chasing fuckhead.'" Holy shit, were they going to make him film a reenactment with Damian?

"So *ossicarminis* brought you together."

"I guess, yeah."

Annika made the hand gesture that meant, *remember to speak in sound bites.* Ray grit his teeth. "*Ossicarminis* brought us together."

"And it broke you apart."

"And it—"

"No, that doesn't scan well." Annika tapped her pen against her lips. "And it *tore* you apart."

Ray took a deep, calming breath, thought of Min being forced to go back to a retail job with her ballooning student debt, and said, "And it tore us apart."

Kamal fist-pumped while Annika smiled beatifically.

***

Min was already at the Cracker Barrel where they'd agreed to meet, nursing a glass of water. She looked better, to be honest—beneath the makeup she'd worn in San Francisco, her exhaustion had been etched onto her entire face. Dissertation year was hell.

"I can't believe you wanted to get dinner somewhere without alcohol," Min said. Ray cursed. He'd wanted to take some petty revenge on Min by making her eat in the most smotheringly homey chain restaurant, but had fucked himself over instead. Story of his goddamn life.

"Yeah, to hell with that. Come on." He jerked his head toward the door. Min shot him a concerned look, but grabbed her sweater and followed him to the Applebee's across the road. He ordered the least expensive cocktail with the highest amount of alcohol, and drank half of it seconds after the waitress set it down on the table.

"Are you okay?" Min asked. He started to bring the glass back toward his mouth, but Min took it out of his hands. "Tell me what happened, and then you can have your Bahama Mama back."

"I told Annika that Damian and I used to fuck." He grimaced. "That we *dated.*" That seemed worse, somehow.

Min blinked. "Okay, so?"

"On camera, during my interview." He put his face in his hands. "I gave *details.*"

Min slid his horrible cocktail back to him. "And you're upset because—"

"Because I really did not want to rehash all of our shit on camera, but it was the first thing I could think of when they asked why I'd stormed off in San Francisco."

Min was silent for so long that he risked a look at her. She was crying.

"Aw, jeez," he said.

"Sorry!" she said. "Sorry, I'm—I don't think anyone has ever taken that big of a bullet for me." She blew her nose on a cocktail napkin. "Also, now that I'm done with grad school, all of my feelings are coming back and I don't remember how to regulate them. I cried during a cat food commercial yesterday."

He dug out his handkerchief and handed it to her.

She took it gingerly and dabbed at her melting mascara. "How are you such an old man?" she asked. "You're only like fifteen years older than me."

"Is having a handkerchief an old man thing?" he asked. He'd always found it handy. It was literally in the name.

Min smiled. "Drink your Bahama Mama so we can go get actual food."

They ended up at a steakhouse on the outskirts of town. Now that the immediate trauma of talking about his sex life on camera had faded, Ray felt able to laugh about it. It helped when Min pointed out that there were small-town queer kids in his classes who would feel a lot better knowing one of their professors was like them.

Min waited until dessert to bring out the wooden box, maybe five inches wide on each side. She slid it across the table to him. "These are for you," she said. "Well, not for *you*, but—"

He didn't need to open them to know what was inside. "The oracle bones?"

Min nodded, the emotions on her face too complicated to pick apart. "I shouldn't have taken them."

Ray rested his fingers on the box, and unable to help himself, he took a look inside it. The three bones were all in there, the *Teratornis* tibias inscribed with the faint, dyed symbols. It was tempting to run his fingers down them, to touch the places where a long-ago neighbor had carved some message worth remembering. But it wasn't written for him.

"Damian said he'd take us to the cave," Min said softly. "If you want to go there tonight." The location of the cave had been kept secret, in order to prevent tourists from overrunning it in the immediate aftermath of the discovery. There were still some weird cults claiming the cave was part of a secret tunnel to the center of the Earth.

"Okay," he said. "You know that's a seven-hour drive from Omaha, right?"

Min's look of horror made him laugh. She was such a city kid. "You can drive for seven hours and *still be in the same state?*"

***

The old dig site hadn't changed much in two years, and Ray felt profoundly grateful for that. It's what they'd fought for, after all.

It was dramatic reenactment day, which, from what Ray could see, seemed to consist of fifteen people (some of whom were pulling double duty as crew members) dressed as either grungy hipsters or suit-wearing corporate guys to yell at each other on camera. It seemed a lot less dramatic than the fight had actually been.

Ray sat with Min in the bed of his truck a safe distance away, both of them watching as Damian dramatically reenacted a confrontation with the Energy and Oil Commission. Damian had a handful of papers and printouts that he would shake in the face of the guys in suits, then theatrically point at something off camera. They had to keep reshooting since the sharp wind kept blowing the papers out of his hands.

"Did this actually happen?" Min asked. She seemed calmer, relaxed and happy. "Like, before I got here, or when I was intently drooling over the oracle bones?"

"Are you kidding? Those guys never left Lincoln."

The wind managed to tug the papers out of Damian's hands again, and they could hear him cursing clear across the field. Ray and Min smiled at each other.

"Should I tell you that you could do better than him?" Min said.

Ray leaned back into his truck. He was a bisexual Indian who got professionally excited about antelope poop, and he lived in a small college town in Kansas. Choices were thin on the ground in Emporia. But to say that he deserved someone better than Damian implied that he also deserved something better than being alone. As if being alone was a punishment. As if there were only one kind of loneliness, and one kind of cure for it.

"You don't have to tell me that," he said. "And you really shouldn't get your mother to tell me that either."

Min pulled out her vape and sucked on it, then exhaled a plume of fruity-smelling vapor. "But he wants you? He gave you a key to his room in San Francisco."

"He said it was in case we got thrown out of the hotel bar because we were arguing so loud." At Min's curious look, he added, "After the museum. You were off hiding somewhere."

"I was *contemplating*," she said grumpily.

"Contemplating punching his lights out?" Ray said with a grin. "That was a sorry-ass fight, by the way. I don't know if I got a chance to tell you."

Min gave him the stink eye. "We're talking about you and Damian."

"I'm not sure what he wants," Ray answered. He thought even Damian wasn't sure what he wanted.

"What do you want?"

"I want those bones back in the ground where they belong." The sun was warm on Ray's skin and clothing, and a burst of wind rocked his truck on its chassis. It had been colder the first time he'd come out here, nearly two years before, like the land was trying to hurry into winter. "Damian doesn't think it's possible, at this point."

Min puffed thoughtfully on her vape. She kept opening her mouth as though she were going to speak, and then closing it around the fancy gizmo instead. It was horrible, but Ray kind of missed the days when people smoked real cigarettes. If you were gonna get some weird cancer in your mouth or lungs or whatever, get it from a plant.

Annika apparently got whatever shot she wanted, and Damian handed off his stack of prop papers to one of the crew. He shouted to them, "You all are up!"

The dramatic reenactment was anything but dramatic. It was, for Ray, a lot of staring into the distance and trying to school his features into an interesting expression, which apparently involved not blinking when the wind threw your hair into your eyes.

"Do you think you can maybe make your face...do something?" Kamal said. Annika was directing Min, who looked like a model, the prairie wind artistically tugging at her hair and scarf.

"Like what?"

"Maybe look less irritated," Damian suggested. He was standing by the monitors.

"I'm standing with the sun in my eyes and being told not to squint," Ray said.

They shot him in a variety of angles and poses, giving him weird, contradictory directions for how to shape his face into something compelling. Thankfully, they didn't ask him to be part of the crowd of extras who were shuffled from place to place with their cardboard signs, prop handcuffs, and performative outrage.

"All right, can we get some chants?" Annika called. "Let's get some chants going, please!"

"What should we chant?" one of them asked.

"It hardly matters," Annika said. "I want to see righteous anger! Righteous!"

Someone started shouting *Hell no, we won't go*, and the words echoed across the empty hills.

"This is so stupid," Ray said to Damian. They were drinking bottled water and eating sandwiches in the craft tent.

"It's for a good cause," Damian offered. He sounded doubtful, and when Ray shot him a look, he wilted a little. "Okay, yeah, it's stupid. But it'll get *ossicarminis* back in the news for a while."

Was that enough? This felt like a desecration of the memory of what they had done, what they had been through. Ray had felt cold, scared, and wildly discombobulated during the months that he'd spent going back and forth between Emporia and this spit of land. They'd worked all hours trying to publicize their findings and keep the Commission from bulldozing the entire dig. What they found should have profoundly moved the world, but it had all...slipped away.

"Is that enough to ask for?" Ray said. "For people to remember that *ossicarminis* exists?"

Damian looked up from his sandwich—just tomatoes and mustard. He must have gone vegan again. "We're going to have trouble doing even that much when we reinter the skeletons."

Ray rolled his eyes, suddenly frustrated with that same stupid argument. "Oh, fuck off, man."

"No, Ray, listen, *listen!*" Damian grabbed the sleeve of his coat. "I've called in every favor I have trying to get the museum to give up the skeletons, or for the state to rebury them. So far, everyone has laughed in my face. This process is going to take years, maybe a decade or more, and it might not work at all."

Ray shook himself free. "So you're telling me that an unpopular demand involving multiple, massive bureaucracies isn't going to be immediately answered? I'm shocked." What was it his students said? "Consider me *shook*."

Damian, it seemed, had not been expecting that level of sarcasm.

"Did you really think we'd get the skeletons back in a couple weeks?" Ray asked. "How the hell did you study archeology and not learn to take the long view on this kind of stuff?"

Damian narrowed his eyes. "I barely graduated and became an activist instead."

"You're telling me you expect immediate payoffs there?" Ray wasn't an activist by any means, but he'd been born in the aftermath of AIM, the siege at Wounded Knee, and Leonard Peltier. They'd discovered *ossicarminis* less than a year after Standing Rock. You learned that surviving as a people meant being more stubborn than your oppressors, getting through one atrocity right as a new one was getting underway.

"A lot of the stuff I got called in for? Like this?" Damian gestured around them. "Is on a timeline of weeks. We were twelve days from getting escorted off the land via water cannons when I found the cave." Damian's face was dark. Ray had forgotten that he'd been out at the site for weeks before he and Min arrived, and from the stories Damian told, the state had been a lot nicer when they realized they were sitting on fossils worth more than shale gas.

"Getting them back in ten years is better than letting them stay where they are forever," Ray said. "You don't give up your dead."

He expected Damian to come after him when he walked away, to stop him and argue with him some more. Ray kept walking, and Damian didn't come after him, so he walked right up to his truck and got into the cab.

***

Yeah, I'm a member of the Sincagu Lakota. I grew up on and around the Rosebud Reservation. Which is actually pretty close to the dig site, maybe a couple hours of driving.

...I guess it was a little like coming home. The landscape felt familiar for sure. The hills and the buttes, pale gray dirt, the pine trees. The wind was the same. The situation—the protests and everything that was going on—that was pretty familiar too. It wasn't bad, though. I'm glad I was there, and I'm proud that we saved that land.

Yes, I am aware of that phrase. No, you don't have to explain what "all my relations" means. No, I'm not going to explain it to you. If you had thirty years, maybe you could understand it. Not in a sound bite.

You just want to hear some deep stuff about ossicarminis and the universe, right? Okay. Picture them, yeah? A species whose last common ancestor diverged from ours, what, a hundred million years ago? But between our ancestors and them, you've got convergent evolution of intelligence, tool manipulation, and language, less than a million years apart and on different continents. We don't know how long they were around, and until two years ago, most white people couldn't conceive of animals showing true intelligence. Some dinguses still can't.

The state of Nebraska was two weeks from completely destroying the last trace of ossicarminis. And for what? For money.

We can't know what ossicarminis thought. We can't translate their messages. We don't know what they thought was important, just that they valued something enough to carve it into bone and bury it with two of their people. We can respect that it was important without having to treat it as, as an episode of Law and Order, you know? We don't have to go all Forensic Files on it.

The two skeletons that Damian found were put there with intent. An adult and a juvenile, maybe a parent and child. Someone mourned them. Someone put them in the earth so they could continue whatever

journey they had started together. We should respect that, both the inten-
tions and the journey.

    ...Good enough? Because I'm not gonna say it again.

***

Ray turned his truck into the long driveway of the Best Value Inn off Highway 71, which the Smithsonian crew had booked for all of them. His room smelled like the set of a porno mixed with cigarettes—not that Ray would really know what a porno set smelled like, but he'd watched enough of them shot in motel rooms like this one that the idea had seeped into his imagination. He turned on the TV to have some noise, pulled off his boots, and lay down on the bed.

He was lonely. He'd been lonely for years, and it wasn't a bad thing. He enjoyed loneliness—courted it, even, with his little ranch house out on the edge of Emporia and his steadfast avoidance of most social media and all but the most necessary department meetings.

He was bored, though. He had a small life that was, at age forty-four, almost certainly half over. He thought he'd do better than his own father, who had died at fifty-eight, but probably not as well as his grandmother, who was still making fry bread and spoiling her misbehaving great-grandkids at eighty-seven.

Maybe that's why, when Damian had slid his keycard across the bar in San Francisco and said they should talk privately, Ray had taken it. Damian had disturbed the comfortable patterns in his life, and Ray—Ray thought he needed a little disturbance now and then.

He pulled out his phone and sent the shortest, hardest text of his life.

Come talk to me.

Of course, asking didn't erase the distance, and it was another hour and a half before there was a knock at the door. Ray started awake; he hadn't meant to sleep, but he'd succumbed less than a minute after lying down on the lumpy mattress. He felt dizzy and disoriented as he pushed himself up and opened the door.

Damian had a tendency to fill a room. He looked claustrophobic framed in the narrow doorway.

"Hi," Ray said. "Come inside."

"Hi," Damian said. He followed him in, looking nervous. He'd changed out of the reenactment getup, which Ray and Min had laughingly called *Indiana Jones and the Sit-In at the Dean's Office*. He wore a flannel shirt that seemed comfortable but too clean, like he was still in a costume, jeans, and an ugly iron pendant on a leather thong.

"So," Damian said.

"Yeah."

They stared at each other.

"I think we should have sex," Ray blurted.

"I think we should create a land trust for the dig site," Damian said, speaking nearly at the same time.

They stared at each other again.

"What?"

"*What?*"

"How would a land trust work?" Ray asked. There was a chunk of trust land north of the Rosebud reservation, but he didn't know much about the particulars.

"What do you mean we should have sex?" Damian said. "I thought—you were all—*when did you decide this?*"

Ray rubbed at the back of his neck, wishing that he hadn't fallen asleep. His brain was still waking up, and it made his words feel awkward and ungainly.

"I miss you?" he said. "And I...miss sex?"

Damian blinked at him, looking confused and increasingly suspicious.

"Can we talk about the land trust?"

"No," Damian said. "We're gonna talk about how you propositioned me."

"I'd really rather—"

"Come talk to me," Damian read off his phone. "Not, *come sit in my room and pretend we're telepathic.*"

Damian sat down on the other bed. Ray sat across from him. "I don't really know what else to say besides that. I miss you. I miss sex."

"When we broke up, you told me that we weren't compatible."

"We're not," Ray said.

"So what do you want with me?" Damian talked with his hands a lot. Right now, he appeared to be screaming with them.

"Okay, let's calm down," Ray said. "You already got into one fistfight."

"It was more like a pillow fight," Damian muttered. "And Min started it."

"Look, I don't want that much. I want to be friends again, though. I miss your...endless texting and commentary about movies I've never watched and never will, and I miss you swearing about politics."

"You want to be *friends,*" Damian said, distressed.

"Why are you saying that like it's a prison sentence? Yeah. I want to be friends."

"Who have sex."

"Sometimes, sure." Ray was blushing and it irritated him. "Why is that weird for you? I thought Millennials were all like, *nbd, no strings attached, whatevs.*" He waved his hands in an approximation of Damian's fluid gestures.

Damian snorted. "Sure, Ray. That's what all the Millennials are saying."

He was making fun of him. It had been a while since Damian had done that. It felt good.

"Now can we talk about the land trust?" Ray said.

"Are you sure you don't want to have sex first?"

Ray opened his mouth to argue, but then reconsidered.

***

You know, I tell my students that there are no stupid questions, but that's a hilariously stupid question. Although I guess it's better than insisting any civilization that wasn't white and European needed help from aliens to get by.

No, I don't think they went into space—at least not the way you're thinking, in a big, shiny, dick-shaped rocket. But who doesn't look at the stars and want to know them better?

I will say that "Space Weasels" would be a pretty cool band name, though.

***

The principle shooting took two more weeks. Ray spent a lot of his off time on the phone with various contacts who had law degrees or worked in public administration, asking them about the process of drawing up a conservation land trust. Damian—despite the fact that he had a much heavier shooting schedule—did the same. Annika, once they told her, fervently promised to get the Smithsonian's institutional support for the project, as well as for the re-interment of the skeletons, which was now the primary focus of the documentary.

"She probably wants to protect the place where *ossicarminis*'s spaceship took off," Ray said with a grin.

Damian huffed. "They've got serious money. I can put up with weirdos if it gets things done."

Ray took a trip up across the state border, to the reservation, to drop off the oracle bones. He left them in the care of another cousin, a medicine man whom he trusted to come up with a good burial ceremony for them. The dig site was on old Lakota land, after all. Much as his family joked about the so-called smart weasels, they were considered kin around the rez.

After their last night of shooting, Annika treated them all to another dinner, this time at a diner in Rapid City, two hours north of the dig site. The waitstaff stared at the enormous group with open hostility, and the food took more than an hour to come out. When it did, Annika stood up and clinked her fork against her enormous plate bearing a lukewarm burger and fries.

"I wanted to say a few words," she boomed. Ray noticed that diners in other booths and tables were craning their heads to look at her. Aliens came in all shapes and forms, he thought. They were all situational aliens.

"As some of you know, this project is one I've been dreaming of for close to a year. I won't say that it's a dream come true, because most of my dreams are disturbing and unsettling. I'm very glad that my dreams remained false." She slowly and purposefully pinched herself on the arm, as if in ritual. Ray shot a quick look of alarm at Damian and Min. Damian was staring fixedly at his plate, very obviously trying not to laugh. Min was filming the whole thing on her phone, probably so she could Snapchat it to her mother.

Annika continued, "I want to thank you. Each of you. All of you." Ray sighed, and submitted himself to the intensity of her stare as she made another forcible round of eye contact.

He, Damian, and Min didn't linger after dinner was finished. The crew had already started making plans to go bar-hopping, but Min waved them off, telling Kamal she'd text him and meet them somewhere in an hour. "We've got an appointment first."

Min cooed at the sight of Ray's truck like she was reuniting with a long-lost pet. "Aw, I've missed the Buttsmobile."

"Burtsmobile, damn it," muttered Ray. He really should have made his nephew pay to fix that leather. That was the problem with making more money than your siblings, though. Nobody could afford for you to be vindictive.

"Just accept that it's the Buttsmobile," Damian said, "and always will be."

"Shotgun!" Min called, and then narrowly beat Damian to the door.

Damian clambered into the middle of the bench seat, squirming to get his seatbelt on. "I hate being short. I always get volunteered to sit in the middle," he grumped. Still, his leg was a comforting weight against Ray's. Heat seeped from his skin where they were pressed together. Min propped one of her boots up on the dash and stretched her other leg down into the footwell. "Window," Ray said as she pulled out her vape.

"It's not even smoke," she complained as she cranked down the window.

"It smells like you're standing between a Garrett's Popcorn and a Claire's Boutique in the mall," Damian said. "That might be worse."

It had been Min's idea to get the tattoos. They'd argued for a while about which of the twenty-nine logograms from the oracles to get, until Ray pointed out that they really didn't need to get matching ones anyway. The tattoos were a reminder.

"A reminder of what?" Damian asked.

"Whatever you want to be reminded of," Ray said.

Min had eventually chosen two mirrored crescents. Damian wanted the fern. Ray picked the lopsided triangle shape that he thought was a bird's wing but Min argued was actually an abstracted symbol.

The tattoo shop was grotty, with stained ceilings and an ugly linoleum floor, and both Damian and Min looked a little squeamish. But the woman behind the counter was using proper sterilization procedures, and that was good enough for Ray.

"What are these from, anyway?" she asked, once she'd started inking Ray's forearm. "Do they mean something?"

"Probably 'thanks for the gift of shiny stones,'" said Min.

"We don't know," Damian answered. "Probably never will. But we know they meant *something*."

"At the very least, it means that someone was there," Ray said. Then he smirked at Damian and added, "Before they flew off into space, anyway."

"Cool cool," replied the artist, who had probably heard much weirder things in her shop. "That's about all any artist can hope for, I guess."

ABOUT THE AUTHOR

Nino Cipri is a queer and nonbinary/transgender writer, currently at work on an MFA at the University of Kansas. A multidisciplinary artist, Nino has also written plays, screenplays, and radio features; performed as a dancer, actor, and puppeteer; and worked as a stagehand, bookseller, bike mechanic, and labor organizer. Their fiction has been published by *Tor.com, Fireside Fiction, Nightmare Magazine*, and other fine venues. One time, an angry person called Nino a verbal terrorist, which was pretty cool.

ACKNOWLEDGMENTS

This book contains about seven years of my writing, but is the result of decades of help, teaching, and support from a dozen different directions. This list is long, sorry not sorry.

Thanks first to Michelle Dotter, Dan Wickett, Catherine Sinow, and everyone else at Dzanc, who chose this from a mountain of submissions for their annual contest. I'm so thrilled that my first book was with people who recognized what I was trying to do and helped me do it better. Michelle in particular was kind, patient, and constantly encouraging throughout the process.

My agent, DongWon Song, is the actual best, and I'm lucky to have him. Thank you for your insight, humor, and for gently suggesting replacements for my terrible titles.

Most of these stories were first published in various SF/F literary magazines, whose editors are absolute champions of the genre and its writers. I'd like to specially shout out John Joseph Adams at *Nightmare/Lightspeed*, Ann VanderMeer of *Tor.com*, and Brian White and Julia Rios of *Fireside*. It's been such a pleasure working with you all.

I've had so many wonderful writing teachers, starting from when I was an insufferable teenager convinced of my own genius. In roughly chronological order, I'd like to thank Jay Craven, Rob Williams, Burgess Clark, Walter Eugene Grodzik, Gail Tremblay, Gregory Frost, Geoff Ryman, Catherynne Valente, Nora Jemisin, Ann VanderMeer, Jeff VanderMeer, Kij Johnson, Laura Moriarty, Darren Canady, and Giselle Anatol.

Writing is lonely sometimes, but I'm lucky to have family and friends who make it less so. Ellen and Leah Cipri, and the whole Cipri clan; Nibedita Sen, best of boos; the best-ever Aunt Squad of Anne Brunelle and Cathy MacIntyre; queerplatonic life-partner k8 Walton; my classmates and cohort at the University of Kansas, especially Hannah Warren, Maria Dones, Kyle Teller, and Jason Baltazar; my classmates at the 2014 Clarion Writing Workshop, who taught me as much as the teachers; and the amazing queer and trans writing family that I've come to know, who are always reminding me to drink more water and believe in my work.

Particular to "Before We Disperse like Star Stuff," which was the last story to be written: Darcie Little Badger was kind enough to talk to me about being an Indigenous scientist. Sisi Jiang, Angeline Rodriguez, and Kyna Horten provided amazing and insightful sensitivity reads. In my research, I came across a lot of work by critics, scientists, researchers, and writers that had a profound impact on the story, including Kim Tallbear, Kara Stewart, Debbie Reese, Adrienne Keene, and Adrienne Mayor.

Lastly, gratitude to various trees in Vermont, Colorado, Washington, Illinois, Kansas, and elsewhere for existing so awesomely that I would stand beneath them and go, *Trees! Wow!* and feel a little better about the world.